WAR DANCES

Also by Sherman Alexie

FICTION
The Absolutely True Diary of a Part-Time Indian
Flight
Ten Little Indians
The Toughest Indian in the World
The Lone Ranger and Tonto Fistfight in Heaven
Indian Killer
Reservation Blues

SCREENPLAYS
The Business of Fancy Dancing
Smoke Signals

POETRY
Face
Dangerous Astronomy
Il powwow della fine del mondo
One Stick Song
The Man Who Loves Salmon
The Summer of Black Widows
Water Flowing Home
Seven Mourning Songs for the Cedar Flute
I Have Yet to Learn to Play
First Indian on the Moon
Old Shirts & New Skins
I Would Steal Horses
The Business of Fancy Dancing

WAR DANCES

by

Sherman Alexie

Grove Press
New York

FIRST EDITION

ISBN 13: 978-0-8021-1919-3

NOV 9 2009
Grove Press
an imprint of Grove/Atlantic, Inc.
841 Broadway
New York, NY 10003

Distributed by Publishers Group West
www.groveatlantic.com

09 10 11 12   10 9 8 7 6 5 4 3 2 1

For
Elisabeth, Morgan, Eric, and Deb

Contents

Contents

WAR DANCES

The Limited

I saw a man swerve his car
And try to hit a stray dog,
But the quick mutt dodged
Between two parked cars

And made his escape.
God, I thought, did I just see
What I think I saw?
At the next red light,

I pulled up beside the man
And stared hard at him.
He knew that'd I seen
His murder attempt,

But he didn't care.
He smiled and yelled loud
Enough for me to hear him
Through our closed windows:

"Don't give me that face
Unless you're going to do
Something about it.
Come on, tough guy,

What are you going to do?"
I didn't do anything.
I turned right on the green.
He turned left against traffic.

I don't know what happened
To that man or the dog,
But I drove home
And wrote this poem.

Why do poets think
They can change the world?
The only life I can save
Is my own.

Breaking and Entering

Back in college, when I was first learning how to edit film—how to construct a scene—my professor, Mr. Baron, said to me, "You don't have to show people using a door to walk into a room. If people are already in the room, the audience will understand that they didn't crawl through a window or drop from the ceiling or just materialize. The audience understands that a door has been used—the eyes and mind will make the connection—so you can just skip the door."

Mr. Baron, a full-time visual aid, skipped as he said, "Skip the door." And I laughed, not knowing that I would always remember his bit of teaching, though of course, when I tell the story now, I turn my emotive professor into the scene-eating lead of a Broadway musical.

"Skip the door, young man!" Mr. Baron sings in my stories— my lies and exaggerations—skipping across the stage with a top hat in one hand and a cane in the other. "Skip the door, old friend! And you will be set free!"

"Skip the door" is a good piece of advice—a maxim, if you will—that I've applied to my entire editorial career, if not my entire life. To state it in less poetic terms, one would say, "An editor must omit all unnecessary information." So in telling you this story—with words, not film or video stock—in constructing its scenes, I will attempt to omit all unnecessary information. But oddly enough, in order to skip the door in telling this story, I am forced to begin with a door: the front door of my home on Twenty-seventh Avenue in the Central District neighborhood of Seattle, Washington.

One year ago, there was a knock on that door. I heard it, but I did not rise from my chair to answer. As a freelance editor, I work at home, and I had been struggling with a scene from a locally made film, an independent. Written, directed, and shot by amateurs, the footage was both incomplete and voluminous. Simply stated, there was far too much of nothing. Moreover, it was a love scene—a graphic sex scene, in fact—and the director and the producer had somehow convinced a naive and ambitious local actress to shoot the scene full frontal, graphically so. This was not supposed to be a pornographic movie; this was to be a tender coming-of-age work of art. But it wasn't artistic, or not the kind of art it pretended to be. This young woman had been exploited—with her permission, of course—but I was still going to do my best to protect her.

Don't get me wrong. I'm not a prude—I've edited and enjoyed sexual and violent films that were far more graphic—but I'd spotted honest transformative vulnerability in that young actress's performance. Though the director and the producer thought she'd just been acting—had created her fear and shame through technical skill—I knew better. And so, by editing out the more gratuitous nudity and focusing on faces and small pieces of dialogue—and by paying more attention to fingertips than to what those fingertips were touching—I was hoping to turn a sleazy gymnastic sex scene into an exchange that resembled how two people in new love might actually touch each other.

Was I being paternalistic, condescending, and hypocritical? Sure. After all, I was being paid to work with exploiters, so didn't that mean I was also being exploited as I helped exploit the woman? And what about the young man, the actor, in the scene? Was he dumb and vulnerable as well? Though he was allowed—was legally bound—to keep his penis hidden, wasn't he more exploited than exploiter? These things are hard to define. Still, even in the most compromised of situations, one must find a moral center.

But how could I find any center with that knocking on the door? It had become an evangelical pounding: *Bang, bang, bang, bang!* It had to be the four/four beat of a Jehovah's Witness or a Mormon. *Bang, cha, bang, cha!* It had to be the iambic pentameter of a Sierra Club shill or a magazine sales kid.

Trust me, nobody interesting or vital has ever knocked on a front door at three in the afternoon, so I ignored the knocking and kept at my good work. And, sure enough, my potential guest stopped the noise and went away. I could hear feet pounding down the stairs and there was only silence—or, rather, the relative silence of my urban neighborhood.

But then, a few moments later, I heard a window shatter in my basement. Is shatter too strong a verb? I heard my window break. But break seems too weak a verb. As I visualize the moment—as I edit in my mind—I add the sound track, or rather I completely silence the sound track. I cut the sounds of the city—the planes overhead, the cars on the streets, the boats on the lake, the televisions and the voices and the music and the wind through the trees—until one can hear only shards of glass dropping onto a hardwood floor.

And then one hears—feels—the epic thump of two feet landing on that same floor.

Somebody—the same person who had knocked on my front door to ascertain if anybody was home, had just broken and entered my life.

Now please forgive me if my tenses—my past, present, and future—blend, but one must understand that I happen to be one editor who is not afraid of jump cuts—of rapid flashbacks and flash-forwards. In order to be terrified, one must lose all sense of time and place. When I heard those feet hit the floor, I traveled back in time—I de-evolved, I suppose—and became a primitive version of myself. I had been a complex organism—but I'd turned into a two-hundred-and-two pound one-celled amoeba. And that amoeba knew only fear.

Looking back, I suppose I should have just run away. I could have run out the front door into the street, or the back door onto the patio, or the side door off the kitchen into the alley, or even through the door into the garage—where I could have dived through the dog door cut into the garage and made my caninelike escape.

But here's the salt of the thing: though I cannot be certain, I believe that I was making my way toward the front door—after all, the front door was the only place in my house where I could be positive that my intruder was *not* waiting. But in order to get from my office to the front door, I had to walk past the basement door. And as I walked past the basement door, I spotted the baseball bat.

It wasn't my baseball bat. Now, when one thinks of baseball bats, one conjures images of huge slabs of ash wielded by steroid-fueled freaks. But that particular bat belonged to my ten-year-old son. It was a Little League bat, so it was comically small. I could easily swing it with one hand and had, in fact, often swung it one-handed as I hit practice grounders to the little second baseman of my heart, my son, my Maximilian, my Max. Yes, I am a father. And a husband. That is information you need to know. My wife, Wendy, and my son were not in the house. To give me the space and time I needed to finish editing the film, my wife had taken our son to visit her mother and father in Chicago; they'd been gone for one week and would be gone for another. So, to be truthful, I was in no sense being forced to defend my family, and I'd never been the kind of man to defend his home, his property, his shit. In fact, I'd often laughed at the news footage of silly men armed with garden hoses as they tried to defend their homes from wildfires. I always figured those men would die, go to hell, and spend the rest of eternity having squirt-gun fights with demons.

So with all that information in mind, why did I grab my son's baseball bat and open the basement door? Why did I creep down the stairs? Trust me, I've spent many long nights awake, asking myself those questions. There are no easy answers. Of course, there are many men—and more than a few women—who believe I was fully within my rights to head down those stairs and confront my intruder. There are laws that define—that frankly encourage—the art of self-defense. But since I wasn't interested in defending my property, and since my family and I were not being directly threatened, what part of my self could I have possibly been defending?

In the end, I think I wasn't defending anything at all. I'm an editor—an artist—and I like to make connections; I am paid to make connections. And so I wonder. Did I walk down those stairs because I was curious? Because a question had been asked (Who owned the feet that landed on my basement floor?) and I, the editor, wanted to discover the answer?

So, yes, slowly I made my way down the stairs and through the dark hallway and turned the corner into our downstairs family room—the man cave, really, with the big television and the pool table—and saw a teenaged burglar. I stood still and silent. Standing with his back to me, obsessed with the task—the crime—at hand, he hadn't yet realized that I was in the room with him.

Let me get something straight. Up until that point I hadn't made any guesses as to the identity of my intruder. I mean, yes, I live in a black neighborhood—and I'm not black—and there had been news of a series of local burglaries perpetrated by black teenagers, but I swear none of that entered my mind. And when I saw him, the burglar, rifling through my DVD collection and shoving selected titles into his backpack—he was a felon with cinematic taste, I guess, and that was a strangely pleasing observation—I didn't think, There's a black teenager stealing from me. I only remembering being afraid and wanting to make my fear go away.

"Get the fuck out of here!" I screamed. "You fucking fucker!"

The black kid was so startled that he staggered into my television—cracking the screen—and nearly fell before he caught his balance and ran for the broken window. I could have—would have—let him make his escape, but he stopped and turned back toward me. Why did he do that? I don't know. He was young and scared and made an irrational decision. Or maybe it wasn't irrational at all. He'd slashed his right hand when he crawled through the broken window, so he must have decided the opening with its jagged glass edges was not a valid or safe exit—who'd ever think a broken window was a proper entry or exit—so he searched for a door. But the door was behind me. He paused, weighed his options, and sprinted toward me. He was going to bulldoze me. Once again, I could have made the decision to avoid conflict and step aside. But I didn't. As that kid ran toward me I swung the baseball bat with one hand.

I often wonder what would have happened if that bat had been made of wood. When Max and I had gone shopping for bats, I'd tried to convince him to let me buy him a wooden one, an old-fashioned slugger, the type I'd used when I was a Little Leaguer. I've always been a nostalgic guy. But my son recognized that a ten-dollar wooden bat purchased at Target was not a good investment.

"That wood one will break easy," Max had said. "I want the lum-a-lum one."

Of course, he'd meant to say *aluminum;* we'd both laughed at his mispronunciation. And I'd purchased the lum-a-lum bat.

So it was a metal bat that I swung one-handed at the black teenager's head. If it had been cheap and wooden, perhaps the bat would have snapped upon contact and dissipated the force. Perhaps. But this bat did not snap. It was strong and sure, so when it made full contact with the kid's temple, he dropped to the floor and did not move.

He was dead. I had killed him.

I fell to my knees next to the kid, dropped my head onto his chest, and wept.

I don't remember much else about the next few hours, but I called 911, opened the door for the police, and led them to the body. And I answered and asked questions.

"Did he have a gun or knife?"

"I don't know. No. Well, I didn't see one."

"He attacked you first?"

"He ran at me. He was going to run me over."

"And that's when you hit him with the bat?"

"Yes. It's my son's bat. It's so small. I can't believe it's strong enough to—is he really dead?"

"Yes."

"Who is he?"

"We don't know yet."

His name was Elder Briggs. Elder: such an unusual name for anybody, especially a sixteen-year-old kid. He was a junior at Garfield High School, a B student and backup point guard for the basketball team, an average kid. A good kid, by all accounts. He had no criminal record—had never committed even a minor infraction in school, at home, or in the community—so why had this good kid broken into my house? Why had he decided to steal from me? Why had he made all the bad decisions that had led to his death?

The investigation was quick but thorough, and I was not charged with any crime. It was self-defense. But then nothing is ever clear, is it? I was legally innocent, that much is true, but was I morally innocent? I wasn't sure, and neither were a significant percentage of my fellow citizens. Shortly after the police held the press conference that exonerated me, Elder's family— his mother, father, older brother, aunts, uncles, cousins, friends, and priest—organized a protest. It was small, only forty or fifty people, but how truly small can a protest feel when you are the subject—the object—of that protest?

I watched the live coverage of the event. My wife and son, after briefly returning from Chicago, had only spent a few days with me before they fled back to her parents. We wanted to protect our child from the media. An ironic wish, considering that the media were only interested in me because I'd killed somebody else's child.

"The police don't care about my son because he's black," Elder's mother, Althea, said to a dozen different microphones and as many cameras. "He's just another black boy killed by a white man. And none of these white men care."

As Althea continued to rant about my whiteness, some clever producer—and his editor—cut into footage of me, the white man who owned a baseball bat, walking out of the police station as a free man. It was a powerful piece of editing. It made me look pale and guilty. But all of them—Althea, the other protesters, the reporters, producers, and editors—were unaware of one crucial piece of information: I am not a white man.

I am an enrolled member of the Spokane Tribe of Indians. Oh, I don't look Indian, or at least not typically Indian. Some folks assume I'm a little bit Italian or Spanish or perhaps Middle Eastern. Most folks think I'm just another white guy who tans well. And since I'd just spent months in a dark editing room, I was at my palest. But I grew up on the Spokane Indian Reservation, the only son of a mother and father who were also Spokane Indians who grew up on our reservation. Yes, both of my grandfathers had been half-white, but they'd both died before I was born.

I'm not trying to be holy here. I wasn't a traditional Indian. I didn't dance or sing powwow or speak my language or spend my free time marching for Indian sovereignty. And I'd married a white woman. One could easily mock my lack of cultural connection, but one could not question my race. That's not true, of course. People, especially other Indians, always doubted my race. And I'd always tried to pretend it didn't matter—I was confident about my identity—but it did hurt my feelings. So when I heard Althea Riggs misidentify my race—and watched the media covertly use editing techniques to confirm her misdiagnosis—I picked up my cell phone and dialed the news station.

"Hello," I said to the receptionist. "This is George Wilson. I'm watching your coverage of the protests and I must issue a correction."

"Wait, what?" the receptionist asked. "Are you really George Wilson?"

"Yes, I am."

"Hold on," she said. "Let me put you straight through to the producer."

So the producer took the call and, after asking a few questions to further confirm my identity, he put me on live. So my voice played over images of Althea Riggs weeping and wailing, of her screaming at the sky, at God. How could I have allowed myself to be placed into such a compromising position? How could I have been such an idiot? How could I have been so goddamn callous and self-centered?

"Hello, Mr. Wilson," the evening news anchor said. "I understand you have something you'd like to say."

"Yes." My voice carried into tens of thousands of Seattle homes. "I am watching the coverage of the protest, and I insist on a correction. I am not a white man. I am an enrolled member of the Spokane Tribe of Indians."

Yes, that was my first official public statement about the death of Elder Briggs. It didn't take clever editing to make me look evil; I had accomplished this in one take, live and uncut.

I was suddenly the most hated man in Seattle. And the most beloved. My fellow liberals spoke of my lateral violence and the destructive influence of colonialism on the indigenous, while conservatives lauded my defensive stand and lonely struggle against urban crime. Local bloggers posted hijacked footage of the most graphically violent films I'd edited.

And finally, a local news program obtained rough footage of the film I'd been working on when Elder Briggs broke into my house. Though I had, through judicious editing, been trying to protect the young actress, a black actress, the news only played the uncut footage of the obviously frightened and confused woman. And when the reporters ambushed her—her name was Tracy—she, of course, could only respond that, yes, she felt as if she'd been violated. I didn't blame her for that; I agreed with her. But none of that mattered. I could in no way dispute the story—the cleverly edited series of short films—

that had been made about me. Yes, I was a victim, but I didn't for one second forget that Elder Briggs was dead. I was ashamed and vilified, but I was alive.

I spent most of that time alone in my basement, in the room where I had killed Elder Briggs. When one spends that much time alone, one ponders. And when one ponders, one creates theories—hypotheses, to explain the world. Oh, hell, forget rationalization; I was pissed, mostly at myself for failing to walk away from a dangerous situation. And I was certainly pissed at the local media, who had become as exploitative as any pornographic moviemaker. But I was also pissed at Althea and Elder Briggs.

Yes, the kid was a decent athlete; yes, the kid was a decent student; yes, the kid was a decent person. But he had broken into my house. He had smashed my window and was stealing my DVDs and, if I had not been home, would have stolen my computer and television and stereo and every other valuable thing in my house. And his mother, Althea, instead of explaining why her good and decent son had broken and entered a stranger's house, committing a felony, had instead decided to blame me and accuse me of being yet another white man who was always looking to maim another black kid—had already maimed generations of black kids—when in fact I was a reservation Indian who had been plenty fucked myself by generations of white men. So, Althea, do you want to get into a pain contest? Do you want to participate in the Genocidal Olympics? Whose tragic history has more breadth and depth and length?

Oh, Althea, why the hell was your son in my house? And oh, my God, it was a *Little League* baseball bat! It was only twenty inches long and weighed less than three pounds. I could have hit one hundred men in the head—maybe one thousand or one million—and not done anything more than given them a head-ache. But on that one day, on that one bitter afternoon, I took a swing—a stupid, one-handed, unlucky cut—and killed a kid, a son, a young man who was making a bad decision but who maybe had brains and heart and soul enough to stop making bad decisions.

Oh, Jesus, I murdered somebody's potential.

Oh, Mary, it was self-defense, but it was still murder. I con-fess: I am a killer.

How does one survive these revelations? One just lives. Or, rather, one just finally walks out of his basement and realizes that the story is over. It's old news. There are new villains and heroes, criminals and victims, to be defined and examined and tossed aside.

Elder Briggs and I were suddenly and equally unimportant.

My life became quiet again. I took a job teaching private-school white teenagers how to edit video. They used their newly developed skills to make documentaries about poor brown people in other countries. It's not oil that runs the world, it's shame. My Max was always going to love me, even when he began to understand my limitations, I didn't know what my wife thought of my weaknesses.

Weeks later, in bed, after lovemaking, she interrogated me.

"Honey," she said.

"Yes," I said.

"Can I ask you something?"

"Anything."

"With that kid, did you lose your temper?"

"What do you mean?" I asked.

"Well, you have lost your temper before."

"Just one time."

"Yes, but you broke your hand when you punched the wall."

"Do you think I lost my temper with Elder Briggs?" I asked.

My wife paused before answering, and in that pause I heard all her doubt and fear. So I got out of bed, dressed, and left the house. I decided to drive to see a hot new independent film—a gory war flick that pretended to be antiwar—but first stepped into a mini-mart to buy candy I could smuggle into the theater.

I was standing in the candy aisle, trying to decide between a PayDay and a Snickers, when a group of young black men walked into the store. They were drunk or high and they were cursing the world, but in a strangely friendly way. How is it that black men can make a word like *motherfucker* sound jovial?

There are people—white folks, mostly—who are extremely uncomfortable in the presence of black people. And I know plenty of Indians—my parents, for example—who are also uncomfortable around black folks. As for me? I suppose I'd always been the kind of nonblack person who celebrated himself for not being uncomfortable around blacks. But now, as I watched those black men jostle one another up and down the aisles, I was afraid—no, I was nervous. What if they recognized me? What if they were friends of Elder Briggs? What if they attacked me?

Nothing happened, of course. Nothing ever really happens, you know. Life is infinitesimal and incremental and inconsequential. Those young black men paid for their energy drinks and left the store. I paid for my candy bar, walked out to my car, and drove toward the movie theater.

One block later, I had to hit my brakes when those same black guys jaywalked across the street in front of me. All of them stared me down and walked as slowly as possible through the crosswalk. I'd lived in this neighborhood for years and I'd often had this same encounter with young black men. It was some remnant of the warrior culture, I suppose.

When it had happened before, I had always made it a point to smile goofily and wave to the black men who were challenging me. Since they thought I was a dorky white guy, I'd behave like one. I'd be what they wanted me to be.

But this time, when those black men walked in slow motion in front of me, I did not smile or laugh. I just stared back at them. I knew I could hit the gas and slam into them and hurt them, maybe even kill them. I knew I had that power. And I knew that I would not use that power. But what about these black guys? What power did they have? They could only make me wait at an intersection. And so I waited. I waited until they walked around the corner and out of my vision. I waited until another driver pulled up behind me and honked his horn. I was supposed to move, and so I went.

Go, Ghost, Go

At this university upon a hill,
      I meet a tenured professor
         Who's strangely thrilled
      To list all of the oppressors—
Past, present, and future—who have killed,
Are killing, and will kill the indigenous.
         O, he names the standard suspects—
           Rich, white, and unjust—
      And I, a red man, think he's correct,
But why does he have to be so humorless?

And how can he, a white man, fondly speak
      Of the Ghost Dance, the strange and cruel
         Ceremony
      That, if performed well, would have doomed
All white men to hell, destroyed their colonies,
And brought every dead Indian back to life?
      The professor says, "Brown people
         From all brown tribes
      Will burn skyscrapers and steeples.
They'll speak Spanish and carry guns and knives.

Sherman, can't you see that immigration
　　　　Is the new and improved Ghost Dance?"
　　　　All I can do is laugh and laugh
And say, "Damn, you've got some imagination.
You should write a screenplay about this shit—
　　　　About some fictional city,
　　　　Grown fat and pale and pretty,
That's destroyed by a Chicano apocalypse."
The professor doesn't speak. He shakes his head
　　　　And assaults me with his pity.
　　　　I wonder how he can believe
In a ceremony that requires his death.
I think that he thinks he's the new Jesus.
　　　　He's eager to get on that cross
　　　　And pay the ultimate cost
Because he's addicted to the indigenous.

Bird-watching at Night

What kind of bird is that?

An owl.

What kind of bird was that?

Another owl.

Oh, that one was too quick and small to be an owl. What was it?

A quick and small owl.

One night, when I was sixteen, I was driving with my girlfriend up on Little Falls Flat and this barn owl swooped down over the road, maybe fifty feet or so in front of us, and came flying straight toward our windshield. It was huge, pterodactyl-size, and my girlfriend screamed. And—well, I screamed, too, because that thing was heading straight for us, but you know what I did? I slammed on the gas and sped toward that owl. Do you know why I did that?

Because you wanted to play chicken with the owl?

Exactly.

So what happened?

When we were maybe a second from smashing into each other, that owl just flapped its wings, but barely. What's a better word than *flap*? What's a word that still means *flap*, but a smaller *flap*?

How about slant?

Oh, yes, that's pretty good. So, like I was saying, as that owl was just about to smash into our windshield, it slanted its wings, and slanted up into the dark. And it was so friggin' amazing, you know? I just slammed on the brakes and nearly slid into the ditch. And my girlfriend and I were sitting there in the dark with the engine *tick, tick, tick*ing like some kind of bomb, but an existential bomb, like it was just measuring out the endless nothingness of our lives because that owl had nearly touched us but was gone forever. And I said something like, "That was magnificent," and my girlfriend—you want to know what she said?

She said something like, "I'm breaking up with you."

Damn, that's exactly what she said. And I asked her, "Why are you breaking up with me?" And do you know what she said?

She said, "I'm breaking up with you because you are not an owl."

Yes, yes, yes, and you know what? I have never stopped thinking about her. It's been twenty-seven years, and I still miss her. Why is that?

Brother, you don't miss her. You miss the owl.

After Building the Lego *Star Wars* Ultimate Death Star

How many planets do you want to destroy?
Don't worry, Daddy, this is just a big toy,
And there is nothing more fun than making noise.

My sons, when I was a boy, I threw dirt clods
And snow grenades stuffed with hidden rocks, and fought
Enemies—other Indian boys—who thought,

Like me, that joyful war turned us into gods.

WAR DANCES

1. My Kafka Baggage

A few years ago, after I returned from a trip to Los Angeles, I unpacked my bag and found a dead cockroach, shrouded by a dirty sock, in a bottom corner. "Shit," I thought. "We're being invaded." And so I threw the unpacked clothes, books, shoes, and toiletries back into the suitcase, carried it out onto the driveway, and dumped the contents onto the pavement, ready to stomp on any other cockroach stowaways. But there was only the one cockroach, stiff and dead. As he lay on the pavement, I leaned closer to him. His legs were curled under his body. His head was tilted at a sad angle. Sad? Yes, sad. For who is lonelier than the cockroach without his tribe? I laughed at myself. I was feeling empathy for a dead cockroach. I wondered about its story. How had it got into my bag? And where? At the hotel in Los Angeles? In an airport baggage system? It didn't originate in our house. We've kept those tiny bastards away from our place for fifteen years. So what had happened to this little vermin? Did he smell something delicious in my bag—my musky deodorant or some crumb of chocolate Power Bar—and climb inside, only to be crushed by the shifts of fate and garment bags? As he died, did he feel fear? Isolation? Existential dread?

2. SYMPTOMS

Last summer, in reaction to various allergies I was suffering from, defensive mucous flooded my inner right ear and confused, frightened, untied, and unmoored me. Simply stated, I could not fucking hear a thing from that side, so I had to turn my head to understand what my two sons, ages eight and ten, were saying.

"We're hungry," they said. "We keep telling you."

They wanted to be fed. And I had not heard them.

"Mom would have fed us by now," they said.

Their mother had left for Italy with her mother two days ago. My sons and I were going to enjoy a boys' week, filled with unwashed socks, REI rock wall climbing, and ridiculous heaps of pasta.

"What are you going to cook?" my sons asked. "Why haven't you cooked yet?"

I'd been lying on the couch reading a book while they played and I had not realized that I'd gone partially deaf. So I, for just a moment, could only weakly blame the silence—no, the contradictory roar that only I could hear.

Then I recalled the man who went to the emergency room because he'd woken having lost most, if not all, of his hearing. The doctor peered into one ear, saw an obstruction, reached in with small tweezers, and pulled out a cockroach, then reached into the other ear, and extracted a much larger cockroach. Did you know that ear wax is a delicacy for roaches?

I cooked dinner for my sons—overfed them out of guilt—and cleaned the hell out of our home. Then I walked into the bathroom and stood close to my mirror. I turned my head and body at weird angles, and tried to see deeply into my congested ear. I sang hymns and prayed that I'd see a small angel trapped in the canal. I would free the poor thing, and she'd unfurl and pat dry her tiny wings, then fly to my lips and give me a sweet kiss for sheltering her metamorphosis.

3. The Symptoms Worsen

When I woke at three a.m., completely unable to hear out of my clogged right ear, and positive that a damn swarm of locusts was wedged inside, I left a message for my doctor, and told him that I would be sitting outside his office when he reported to work.

This would be the first time I had been inside a health-care facility since my father's last surgery.

4. Blankets

After the surgeon cut off my father's right foot—no, half of my father's right foot—and three toes from the left, I sat with him in the recovery room. It was more like a recovery hallway. There was no privacy, not even a thin curtain. I guessed it made it easier for the nurses to monitor the postsurgical patients, but still, my father was exposed—his decades of poor health and worse decisions were illuminated—on white sheets in a white hallway under white lights.

"Are you okay?" I asked. It was a stupid question. Who could be okay after such a thing? Yesterday, my father had *walked* into the hospital. Okay, he'd shuffled while balanced on two canes, but that was still called walking. A few hours ago, my father still had both of his feet. Yes, his feet and toes had been black with rot and disease but they'd still been, technically speaking, feet and toes. And, most important, those feet and toes had belonged to my father. But now they were gone, sliced off. Where were they? What did they do with the right foot and the toes from the left foot? Did they throw them in the incinerator? Were their ashes floating over the city?

"Doctor, I'm cold," my father said.

"Dad, it's me," I said.

"I know who are you. You're my son." But considering the blankness in my father's eyes, I assumed he was just guessing at my identity.

"Dad, you're in the hospital. You just had surgery."

"I know where I am. I'm cold."

"Do you want another blanket?" Another stupid question. Of course, he wanted another blanket. He probably wanted me to build a fucking campfire or drag in one of those giant propane heaters that NFL football teams used on the sidelines.

I walked down the hallway—the recovery hallway—to the nurses' station. There were three women nurses, two white and one black. Being Native American-Spokane and Coeur d'Alene Indian, I hoped my darker pigment would give me an edge with the black nurse, so I addressed her directly.

"My father is cold," I said. "Can I get another blanket?"

The black nurse glanced up from her paperwork and regarded me. Her expression was neither compassionate nor callous.

"How can I help you, sir?" she asked.

"I'd like another blanket for my father. He's cold."

"I'll be with you in a moment, sir."

She looked back down at her paperwork. She made a few notes. Not knowing what else to do, I stood there and waited.

"Sir," the black nurse said. "I'll be with you in a moment."

She was irritated. I understood. After all, how many thousands of times had she been asked for an extra blanket? She was a nurse, an educated woman, not a damn housekeeper. And it was never really about an extra blanket, was it? No, when people asked for an extra blanket, they were asking for a time machine. And, yes, she knew she was a health care provider, and she knew she was supposed to be compassionate, but my father, an alcoholic, diabetic Indian with terminally damaged kidneys, had just endured an incredibly expensive surgery for what? So he could ride his motorized wheelchair to the bar and win bets by showing off his disfigured foot? I know she didn't want to be cruel, but she believed there was a point when doctors should stop rescuing people from their own self-destructive impulses. And I couldn't disagree with her but I could ask for the most basic of comforts, couldn't I?

"My father," I said. "An extra blanket, please."

"Fine," she said, then stood and walked back to a linen closet, grabbed a white blanket, and handed it to me. "If you need anything else—"

I didn't wait around for the end of her sentence. With the blanket in hand, I walked back to my father. It was a thin blanket, laundered and sterilized a hundred times. In fact, it was too thin. It wasn't really a blanket. It was more like a large beach towel. Hell, it wasn't even good enough for that. It was more like the world's largest coffee filter. Jesus, had health care finally come to this? Everybody was uninsured and unblanketed.

"Dad, I'm back."

He looked so small and pale lying in that hospital bed. How had that change happened? For the first sixty-seven years of his life, my father had been a large and dark man. And now, he was just another pale and sick drone in a hallway of pale and sick drones. A hive, I thought, this place looks like a beehive with colony collapse disorder.

"Dad, it's me."

"I'm cold."

"I have a blanket."

As I draped it over my father and tucked it around his body, I felt the first sting of grief. I'd read the hospital literature about this moment. There would come a time when roles would reverse and the adult child would become the caretaker of the ill parent. The circle of life. Such poetic bullshit.

"I can't get warm," my father said. "I'm freezing."

"I brought you a blanket, Dad, I put it on you."

"Get me another one. Please. I'm so cold. I need another blanket."

I knew that ten more of these cheap blankets wouldn't be enough. My father needed a real blanket, a good blanket.

I walked out of the recovery hallway and made my way through various doorways and other hallways, peering into the rooms, looking at the patients and their families, looking for a particular kind of patient and family.

I walked through the ER, cancer, heart and vascular, neuro-science, orthopedic, women's health, pediatrics, and surgical services. Nobody stopped me. My expression and posture were that of a man with a sick father and so I belonged.

And then I saw him, another Native man, leaning against a wall near the gift shop. Well, maybe he was Asian; lots of those in Seattle. He was a small man, pale brown, with muscular arms and a soft belly. Maybe he was Mexican, which is really a kind of Indian, too, but not the kind that I needed. It was hard to tell sometimes what people were. Even brown people guessed at the identity of other brown people.

"Hey," I said.

"Hey," the other man said.

"You Indian?" I asked.

"Yeah."

"What tribe?"

"Lummi."

"I'm Spokane."

"My first wife was Spokane. I hated her."

"My first wife was Lummi. She hated me."

We laughed at the new jokes that instantly sounded old.

"Why are you in here?" I asked.

"My sister is having a baby," he said. "But don't worry, it's not mine."

"Ayyyyyy," I said—another Indian idiom—and laughed.

"I don't even want to be here," the other Indian said. "But my dad started, like, this new Indian tradition. He says it's a thousand years old. But that's bullshit. He just made it up to impress himself. And the whole family just goes along, even when we know it's bullshit. He's in the delivery room waving eagle feathers around. Jesus."

"What's the tradition?"

"Oh, he does a naming ceremony right in the hospital. Like, it's supposed to protect the baby from all the technology and shit. Like hospitals are the big problem. You know how many babies died before we had good hospitals?"

"I don't know."

"Most of them. Well, shit, a lot of them, at least."

This guy was talking out of his ass. I liked him immediately.

"I mean," the guy said. "You should see my dad right now. He's pretending to go into this, like, fucking trance and is dancing around my sister's bed, and he says he's trying to, you know, see into her womb, to see who the baby is, to see its true nature, so he can give it a name—a protective name—before it's born."

The guy laughed and threw his head back and banged it on the wall.

"I mean, come on, I'm a loser," he said and rubbed his sore skull. "My whole family is filled with losers."

The Indian world is filled with charlatans, men and women who pretended—hell, who might have come to believe—that they were holy. Last year, I had gone to a lecture at the University of Washington. An elderly Indian woman, a Sioux writer and scholar and charlatan, had come to orate on Indian sovereignty and literature. She kept arguing for some kind of separate indigenous literary identity, which was ironic considering that she was speaking English to a room full of white professors. But I wasn't angry with the woman, or even bored. No, I felt sorry for her. I realized that she was dying of nostalgia. She had taken nostalgia as her false idol—her thin blanket—and it was murdering her.

"Nostalgia," I said to the other Indian man in the hospital.

"What?"

"Your dad, he sounds like he's got a bad case of nostalgia."

"Yeah, I hear you catch that from fucking old high school girlfriends," the man said. "What the hell you doing here anyway?"

"My dad just got his feet cut off," I said.

"Diabetes?"

"And vodka."

"Vodka straight up or with a nostalgia chaser?"

"Both."

"Natural causes for an Indian."

"Yep."

There wasn't much to say after that.

"Well, I better get back," the man said. "Otherwise, my dad might wave an eagle feather and change my name."

"Hey, wait," I said.

"Yeah?"

"Can I ask you a favor?"

"What?"

"My dad, he's in the recovery room," I said. "Well, it's more like a hallway, and he's freezing, and they've only got these shitty little blankets, and I came looking for Indians in the hospital because I figured—well, I guessed if I found any Indians, they might have some good blankets."

"So you want to borrow a blanket from us?" the man asked.

"Yeah."

"Because you thought some Indians would just happen to have some extra blankets lying around?"

"Yeah."

"That's fucking ridiculous."

"I know."

"And it's racist."

"I know."

"You're stereotyping your own damn people."

"I know."

"But damn if we don't have a room full of Pendleton blankets. New ones. Jesus, you'd think my sister was having, like, a dozen babies."

Five minutes later, carrying a Pendleton Star Blanket, the Indian man walked out of his sister's hospital room, accompanied by his father, who wore Levi's, a black T-shirt, and eagle feathers in his gray braids.

"We want to give your father this blanket," the old man said. "It was meant for my grandson, but I think it will be good for your father, too."

"Thank you."

"Let me bless it. I will sing a healing song for the blanket. And for your father."

I flinched. This guy wanted to sing a song? That was dangerous. This song could take two minutes or two hours. It was impossible to know. Hell, considering how desperate this old man was to be seen as holy, he might sing for a week. I couldn't let this guy begin his song without issuing a caveat.

"My dad," I said. "I really need to get back to him. He's really sick."

"Don't worry," the old man said and winked. "I'll sing one of my short ones."

Jesus, who'd ever heard of a self-aware fundamentalist? The son, perhaps not the unbeliever he'd pretended to be, sang backup as his father launched into his radio-friendly honor song, just three-and-a-half minutes, like the length of any Top 40 rock song of the last fifty years. But here's the funny thing: the old man couldn't sing very well. If you were going to have the balls to sing healing songs in hospital hallways, then you should logically have a great voice, right? But, no, this guy couldn't keep the tune. And his voice cracked and wavered. Does a holy song lose its power if its singer is untalented?

"That is your father's song," the old man said when he was finished. "I give it to him. I will never sing it again. It belongs to your father now."

Behind his back, the old man's son rolled his eyes and walked back into his sister's room.

"Okay, thank you," I said. I felt like an ass, accepting the blanket and the old man's good wishes, but silently mocking them at the same time. But maybe the old man did have some power, some real medicine, because he peeked into my brain.

"It doesn't matter if you believe in the healing song," the old man said. "It only matters that the blanket heard."

"Where have you been?" my father asked when I returned. "I'm cold."

"I know, I know," I said. "I found you a blanket. A good one. It will keep you warm."

I draped the Star Blanket over my father. He pulled the thick wool up to his chin. And then he began to sing. It was a healing song, not the same song that I had just heard, but a healing song nonetheless. My father could sing beautifully. I wondered if it was proper for a man to sing a healing song for himself. I wondered if my father needed help with the song. I hadn't sung for many years, not like that, but I joined him. I knew this song would not bring back my father's feet. This song would not repair my father's bladder, kidneys, lungs, and heart. This song would not prevent my father from drinking a bottle of vodka as soon as he could sit up in bed. This song would not defeat death. No, I thought, this song is temporary, but right now, temporary is good enough. And it was a good song. Our voices filled the recovery hallway. The sick and healthy stopped to listen. The nurses, even the remote black one, unconsciously took a few steps toward us. The black nurse sighed and smiled. I smiled back. I knew what she was thinking. Sometimes, even after all of these years, she could still be surprised by her work. She still marveled at the infinite and ridiculous faith of other people.

5. DOCTOR'S OFFICE

I took my kids with me to my doctor, a handsome man—a reservist—who'd served in both Iraq wars. I told him I could not hear. He said his nurse would likely have to clear wax and fluid, but when he scoped inside, he discovered nothing.

"Nope, it's all dry in there," he said.

He led my sons and me to the audiologist in the other half of the building. I was scared, but I wanted my children to remain calm, so I tried to stay measured. More than anything, I wanted my wife to materialize.

During the hearing test, I heard only 30 percent of the clicks, bells, and words—I apparently had nerve and bone conductive deafness. My inner ear thumped and thumped.

How many cockroaches were in my head?

My doctor said, "We need an MRI of your ear and brain, and maybe we'll find out what's going on."

Maybe? That word terrified me.

What the fuck was wrong with my fucking head? Had my hydrocephalus come back for blood? Had my levees burst? Was I going to flood?

6. HYDROCEPHALUS

Merriam-Webster's dictionary defines hydrocephalus as "an abnormal increase in the amount of cerebrospinal fluid within the cranial cavity that is accompanied by expansion of the cerebral ventricles, enlargement of the skull and especially the forehead, and atrophy of the brain." I define hydrocephalus as "the obese, imperialistic water demon that nearly killed me when I was six months old."

In order to save my life, and stop the water demon, I had brain surgery in 1967 when I was six months old. I was supposed to die. Obviously, I didn't. I was supposed to be severely mentally disabled. I have only minor to moderate brain damage. I was supposed to have epileptic seizures. Those I did have, until I was seven years old. I was on phenobarbital, a major league antiseizure medication, for six years.

Some of the side effects of phenobarbital—all of which I suffered to some degree or another as a child—include sleepwalking, agitation, confusion, depression, nightmares, hallucinations, insomnia, apnea, vomiting, constipation, dermatitis, fever, liver and bladder dysfunction, and psychiatric disturbance.

How do you like them cockroaches?

And now, as an adult, thirty-three years removed from phenobarbital, I still suffer—to one degree or another—from sleepwalking, agitation, confusion, depression, nightmares, hallucinations, insomnia, bladder dysfunction, apnea, and dermatitis.

Is there such a disease as post-phenobarbital traumatic stress syndrome?

Most hydrocephalics are shunted. A shunt is essentially brain plumbing that drains away excess cerebrospinal fluid. Those shunts often fuck up and stop working. I know hydrocephalics who've had a hundred or more shunt revisions and repairs. That's over a hundred brain surgeries. There are ten fingers on any surgeon's hand. There are two or three surgeons working on any particular brain. That means certain hydrocephalics have had their brains fondled by three thousand fingers.

I'm lucky. I was only temporarily shunted. And I hadn't suffered any hydrocephalic symptoms since I was seven years old.

And then, in July 2008, at the age of forty-one, I went deaf in my right ear.

7. CONVERSATION

Sitting in my car in the hospital parking garage, I called my brother-in-law, who was babysitting my sons.

"Hey, it's me. I just got done with the MRI on my head."

My brother-in-law said something unintelligible. I realized I was holding my cell to my bad ear. And switched it to the good ear.

"The MRI dude didn't look happy," I said.

"That's not good," my brother-in-law said.

"No, it's not. But he's just a tech guy, right? He's not an expert on brains or anything. He's just the photographer, really. And he doesn't know anything about ears or deafness or anything, I don't think. Ah, hell, I don't know what he knows. I just didn't like the look on his face when I was done."

"Maybe he just didn't like you."

"Well, I got worried when I told him I had hydrocephalus when I was a baby and he didn't seem to know what that was."

"Nobody knows what that is."

"That's the truth. Have you fed the boys dinner?"

"Yeah, but I was scrounging. There's not much here."

"I better go shopping."

"Are you sure? I can do it if you need me to. I can shop the shit out of Trader Joe's."

"No, it'll be good for me. I feel good. I fell asleep during the MRI. And I kept twitching. So we had to do it twice. Otherwise, I would've been done earlier."

"That's okay; I'm okay; the boys are okay"

"You know, before you go in that MRI tube, they ask you what kind of music you want to listen to—jazz, classical, rock, or country—and I remembered how my dad spent a lot of time in MRI tubes near the end of his life. So I was wondering what kind of music he always chose. I mean, he couldn't hear shit anyway by that time, but he still must have chosen something. And I wanted to choose the same thing he chose. So I picked country."

"Was it good country?"

"It was fucking Shania Twain and Faith Hill shit. I was hoping for George Jones or Loretta Lynn, or even some George Strait. Hell, I would've cried if they'd played Charley Pride or Freddy Fender."

"You wanted to hear the alcoholic Indian father jukebox."

"Hey, that's my line. You can't quote me to me."

"Why not? You're always quoting you to you."

"Kiss my ass. So, hey, I'm okay, I think. And I'm going to the store. But I think I already said that. Anyway, I'll see you in a bit. You want anything?"

"Ah, man, I love Trader Joe's. But you know what's bad about them? You fall in love with something they have—they stock it for a year—and then it just disappears. They had those wontons I loved and now they don't. I was willing to shop for you and the boys, but I don't want anything for me. I'm on a one-man hunger strike against them."

8. WORLD PHONE CONVERSATION, 3 A.M.

After I got home with yogurt and turkey dogs and Cinnamon Toast Crunch and my brother-in-law had left, I watched George Romero's *Diary of the Dead*, and laughed at myself for choosing a movie that featured dozens of zombies getting shot in the head.

When the movie was over, I called my wife, nine hours ahead in Italy.

"I should come home," she said.

"No, I'm okay," I said. "Come on, you're in Rome. What are you seeing today?"

"The Vatican."

"You can't leave now. You have to go and steal something. It will be revenge for every Indian. Or maybe you can plant an eagle feather and claim that you just discovered Catholicism."

"I'm worried."

"Yeah, Catholicism has always worried me."

"Stop being funny. I should see if I can get Mom and me on a flight tonight."

"No, no, listen, your mom is old. This might be her last adventure. It might be your last adventure with her. Stay there. Say Hi to the Pope for me. Tell him I like his shoes."

That night, my sons climbed into bed with me. We all slept curled around one another like sled dogs in a snowstorm. I woke, hour by hour, and touched my head and neck to check if they had changed shape—to feel if antennae were growing. Some insects "hear" with their antennae. Maybe that's what was happening to me.

9. Valediction

My father, a part-time blue collar construction worker, died in March 2003, from full-time alcoholism. On his deathbed, he asked me to "Turn down that light, please."

"Which light?" I asked.

"The light on the ceiling."

"Dad, there's no light."

"It burns my skin, son. It's too bright. It hurts my eyes."

"Dad, I promise you there's no light."

"Don't lie to me, son, it's God passing judgment on Earth."

"Dad, you've been an atheist since '79. Come on, you're just remembering your birth. On your last day, you're going back to your first."

"No, son, it's God telling me I'm doomed. He's using the brightest lights in the universe to show me the way to my flame-filled tomb."

"No, Dad, those lights were in your delivery room."

"If that's true, son, then turn down my mother's womb."

We buried my father in the tiny Catholic cemetery on our reservation. Since I am named after him, I had to stare at a tombstone with my name on it.

10. Battle Fatigue

Two months after my father's death, I began research on a book about our family's history with war. I had a cousin who had served as a cook in the first Iraq war in 1991; I had another cousin who served in the Vietnam War in 1964–65, also as a cook; and my father's father, Adolph, served in WWII and was killed in action on Okinawa Island, on April 5, 1946.

During my research, I interviewed thirteen men who'd served with my cousin in Vietnam but could find only one surviving man who'd served with my grandfather. This is a partial transcript of that taped interview, recorded with a microphone and an iPod on January 14, 2008:

Me: Ah, yes, hello, I'm here in Livonia, Michigan, to interview—well, perhaps you should introduce yourself, please?

Leonard Elmore: What?

Me: Um, oh, I'm sorry, I was asking if you could perhaps
introduce yourself.

LE: You're going to have to speak up. I think my hearing
aid is going low on power or something.

Me: That is a fancy thing in your ear.

LE: Yeah, let me mess with it a bit. I got a remote control
for it. I can listen to the TV, the stereo, and the telephone with
this thing. It's fancy. It's one of them blue tooth hearing aids.
My grandson bought it for me. Wait, okay, there we go. I can
hear now. So what were you asking?

Me: I was hoping you could introduce yourself into my re-
corder here.

LE: Sure, my name is Leonard Elmore.

Me: How old are you?

LE: I'm eighty-five-and-a-half years old (laughter). My
great-grandkids are always saying they're seven-and-a-half or
nine-and-a-half or whatever. It just cracks me up to say the
same thing at my age.

Me: So, that's funny, um, but I'm here to ask you some
questions about my grandfather—

LE: Adolph. It's hard to forget a name like that. An Indian named Adolph and there was that Nazi bastard named Adolph. Your grandfather caught plenty of grief over that. But we mostly called him "Chief," did you know that?

Me: I could have guessed.

LE: Yeah, nowadays, I suppose it isn't a good thing to call an Indian "Chief," but back then, it was what we did. I served with a few Indians. They didn't segregate them Indians, you know, not like the black boys. I know you aren't supposed to call them boys anymore, but they were boys. All of us were boys, I guess. But the thing is, those Indian boys lived and slept and ate with us white boys. They were right there with us. But, anyway, we called all them Indians "Chief." I bet you've been called "Chief" a few times yourself.

Me: Just once.

LE: Were you all right with it?

Me: I threw a basketball in the guy's face.

LE: (laughter)

Me: We live in different times.

LE: Yes, we do. Yes, we do.

Me: So, perhaps you could, uh, tell me something about my grandfather.

LE: I can tell you how he died.

Me: Really?

LE: Yeah, it was on Okinawa, and we hit the beach, and, well, it's hard to talk about it—it was the worst thing—it was Hell—no, that's not even a good way to describe it. I'm not a writer like you—I'm not a poet—so I don't have the words—but just think of it this way—that beach, that island—was filled with sons and fathers—men who loved and were loved—American and Japanese and Okinawan—and all of us were dying—were being killed by other sons and fathers who also loved and were loved.

Me: That sounds like poetry—tragic poetry—to me.

LE: Well, anyway, it was like that. Fire everywhere. And two of our boys—Jonesy and O'Neal—went down—were wounded in the open on the sand. And your grandfather—who was just this little man—barely five feet tall and maybe one hundred and thirty pounds—he just ran out there and picked up those two guys—one on each shoulder—and carried them to cover. Hey, are you okay, son?

Me: Yes, I'm sorry. But, well, the thing is, I knew my grandfather was a war hero—he won twelve medals—but I could never find out what he did to win the medals.

LE: I didn't know about any medals. I just know what I saw. Your grandfather saved those two boys, but he got shot in the back doing it. And he laid there in the sand—I was lying right beside him—and he died.

Me: Did he say anything before he died?

LE: Hold on. I need to—

49

Me: Are you okay?

LE: It's just—I can't—

Me: I'm sorry. Is there something wrong?

LE: No, it's just—with your book and everything—I know you want something big here. I know you want something big from your grandfather. I knew you hoped he'd said something huge and poetic, like maybe something you could have written, and, honestly, I was thinking about lying to you. I was thinking about making up something as beautiful as I could. Something about love and forgiveness and courage and all that. But I couldn't think of anything good enough. And I didn't want to lie to you. So I have to be honest and say that your grandfather didn't say anything. He just died there in the sand. In silence.

11. ORPHANS

I was worried that I had a brain tumor. Or that my hydrocephalus had returned. I was scared that I was going to die and orphan my sons. But, no, their mother was coming home from Italy. No matter what happened to me, their mother would rescue them.

"I'll be home in sixteen hours," my wife said over the phone.

"I'll be here," I said. "I'm just waiting on news from my doctor."

12. COFFEE SHOP NEWS

While I waited, I asked my brother-in-law to watch the boys again because I didn't want to get bad news with them in the room.

Alone and haunted, I wandered the mall, tried on new clothes, and waited for my cell phone to ring.

Two hours later, I was uncomposed and wanted to murder everything, so I drove south to a coffee joint, a spotless place called Dirty Joe's.

Yes, I was silly enough to think that I'd be calmer with a caffeinated drink.

As I sat outside on a wooden chair and sipped my coffee, I cursed the vague, rumbling, ringing noise in my ear. And yet, when my cell phone rang, I held it to my deaf ear.

"Hello, hello," I said and wondered if it was a prank call, then remembered and switched the phone to my left ear.

"Hello," my doctor said. "Are you there?"

"Yes," I said. "So, what's going on?"

"There are irregularities in your head."

"My head's always been wrong,"

"It's good to have a sense of humor," my doctor said. "You have a small tumor that is called a meningioma. They grow in the meninges membranes that lie between your brain and your skull."

"Shit," I said. "I have cancer."

"Well," my doctor said. "These kinds of tumors are usually noncancerous. And they grow very slowly, so in six months or so, we'll do another MRI. Don't worry. You're going to be okay."

"What about my hearing?" I asked.

"We don't know what might be causing the hearing loss, but you should start a course of prednisone, the steroid, just to go with the odds. Your deafness might lessen if left alone, but we've had success with the steroids in bringing back hearing. There *are* side effects, like insomnia, weight gain, night sweats, and depression."

"Oh, boy," I said. "Those side effects might make up most of my personality already. Will the 'roids also make me quick to pass judgment? And I've always wished I had a dozen more skin tags and moles."

The doctor chuckled. "You're a funny man."

I wanted to throw my phone into a wall but I said good-bye instead and glared at the tumorless people and their pretty tumorless heads.

13. MENINGIOMA

Mayoclinic.com defines "meningioma" as "a tumor that arises from the meninges—the membranes that surround your brain and spinal cord. The majority of meningioma cases are noncancerous (benign), though rarely a meningioma can be cancerous (malignant)."

Okay, that was a scary and yet strangely positive definition. No one ever wants to read the word "malignant" unless one is reading a Charles Dickens novel about an evil landlord, but "benign" and "majority" are two things that go great together.

From the University of Washington Medical School Web site I learned that meningioma tumors "are usually benign, slow growing and do not spread into normal brain tissue. Typically, a meningioma grows inward, causing pressure on the brain or spinal cord. It may grow outward toward the skull, causing it to thicken."

So, wait, what the fuck? A meningioma can cause pressure on the brain and spinal fluid? Oh, you mean, just like fucking hydrocephalus? Just like the water demon that once tried to crush my brain and kill me? Armed with this new information—with these new questions—I called my doctor.

"Hey, you're okay," he said. "We're going to closely monitor you. And your meningioma is very small."

"Okay, but I just read—"

"Did you go on the Internet?"

"Yes."

"Which sites?"

"Mayo Clinic and the University of Washington."

"Okay, so those are pretty good sites. Let me look at them."

I listened to my doctor type.

"Okay, those are accurate," he said.

"What do you mean by accurate?" I asked. "I mean, the whole pressure on the brain thing, that sounds like hydrocephalus."

"Well, there were some irregularities in your MRI that were the burr holes from your surgery and there seems to be some scarring and perhaps you had an old concussion, but other than that, it all looks fine."

"But what about me going deaf? Can't these tumors make you lose hearing?"

"Yes, but only if they're located near an auditory nerve. And your tumor is not."

"Can this tumor cause pressure on my brain?"

"It could, but yours is too small for that."

"So, I'm supposed to trust you on the tumor thing when you can't figure out the hearing thing?"

"The MRI revealed the meningioma, but that's just an image. There is no physical correlation between your deafness and the tumor. Do the twenty-day treatment of Prednisone and the audiologist and I will examine your ear, and your hearing. Then, if there's no improvement, we'll figure out other ways of treating you."

"But you won't be treating the tumor?"

"Like I said, we'll scan you again in six to nine months—"

"You said six before."

"Okay, in six months we'll take another MRI, and if it has grown significantly—or has changed shape or location or anything dramatic—then we'll talk about treatment options. But if you look on the Internet, and I know you're going to spend a lot of time obsessing on this—as you should—I'll tell you what you'll find. About 5 percent of the population has these things and they live their whole lives with these undetected meningiomas. And they can become quite large—without any side effects—and are only found at autopsies conducted for other causes of death. And even when these kinds of tumors become invasive or dangerous they are still rarely fatal. And your tumor, even if it grows fairly quickly, will not likely become an issue for many years, decades. So that's what I can tell you right now. How are you feeling?"

"Freaked and fucked."

I wanted to feel reassured, but I had a brain tumor. How does one feel any optimism about being diagnosed with a brain tumor? Even if that brain tumor is neither cancerous nor interested in crushing one's brain?

14. Drugstore Indian

In Bartell's Drugs, I gave the pharmacist my prescription for Prednisone.

"Is this your first fill with us?" she asked.

"No," I said. "And it won't be the last."

I felt like an ass, but she looked bored.

"It'll take thirty minutes," she said, "more or less. We'll page you over the speakers."

I don't think I'd ever felt weaker, or more vulnerable, or more absurd. I was the weak antelope in the herd—yeah, the mangy fucker with the big limp and a sign that read, "Eat me! I'm a gimp!"

So, for thirty minutes, I walked through the store and found myself shoving more and more useful shit into my shopping basket, as if I were filling my casket with the things I'd need in the afterlife. I grabbed toothpaste, a Swiss Army knife, moisturizer, mouthwash, non-stick Band-Aids, antacid, protein bars, and extra razor blades. I grabbed pen and paper. And I also grabbed an ice scraper and sunscreen. Who can predict what weather awaits us in Heaven?

This random shopping made me feel better for a few minutes but then I stopped and walked to the toy aisle. My boys needed gifts: Lego cars or something, for a lift, a shot of capitalistic joy. But the selection of proper toys is art and science. I have been wrong as often as right and heard the sad song of a disappointed son.

Shit, if I died, I knew my sons would survive, even thrive, because of their graceful mother.

I thought of my father's life: he was just six when his father was killed in World War II. Then his mother, ill with tuberculosis, died a few months later. Six years old, my father was cratered. In most ways, he never stopped being six. There was no religion, no magic tricks, and no song or dance that helped my father.

Jesus, I needed a drink of water, so I found the fountain and drank and drank until the pharmacist called my name.

"Have you taken these before?" she asked.

"No," I said, "but they're going to kick my ass, aren't they?"

That made the pharmacist smile, so I felt sadly and briefly worthwhile. But another customer, some nosy hag, said, "You've got a lot of sleepless nights ahead of you."

I was shocked. I stammered, glared at her, and said, "Miss, how is this any of your business? Please, just fuck all the way off, okay?"

She had no idea what to say, so she just turned and walked away and I pulled out my credit card and paid far too much for my goddamn steroids, and forgot to bring the toys home to my boys.

15. Exit Interview for My Father

- True or False?: when a reservation-raised Native American dies of alcoholism it should be considered death by natural causes.

- Do you understand the term *wanderlust*, and if you do, can you please tell us, in twenty-five words or less, what place made you wanderlust the most?
- Did you, when drunk, ever get behind the tattered wheel of a '76 Ford three-speed van and somehow drive your family one thousand miles on an empty tank of gas?
- Is it true that the only literary term that has any real meaning in the Native American world is *road movie*?
- During the last road movie you saw, how many times did the characters ask, "Are we there yet?"
- How many times, during any of your road trips, did your children ask, "Are we there yet?"
- In twenty-five words or less, please define *there*.
- Sir, in your thirty-nine years as a parent, you broke your children's hearts, collectively and individually, 612 times and you did this without ever striking any human being in anger. Does this absence of physical violence make you a better man than you might otherwise have been?
- Without using the words *man* or *good*, can you please define what it means to be a good man?
- Do you think you will see angels before you die? Do you think angels will come to escort you to Heaven? As the angels are carrying you to Heaven, how many times will you ask, "Are we there yet?"
- Your son distinctly remembers stopping once or twice a month at that grocery store in Freeman, Washington, where you would buy him a red-white-and-blue rocket popsicle and purchase for yourself a pickled pig foot. Your son

distinctly remembers the feet still had their toenails and little tufts of pig fur. Could this be true? Did you actually eat such horrendous food?

- Your son has often made the joke that you were the only Indian of your generation who went to Catholic school on purpose. This is, of course, a tasteless joke that makes light of the forced incarceration and subsequent physical, spiritual, cultural, and sexual abuse of tens of thousands of Native American children in Catholic and Protestant boarding schools. In consideration of your son's questionable judgment in telling jokes, do you think there should be any moral limits placed on comedy?
- Your oldest son and your two daughters, all over thirty-six years of age, still live in your house. Do you think this is a lovely expression of tribal culture? Or is it a symptom of extreme familial codependence? Or is it both things at the same time?
- F. Scott Fitzgerald wrote that the sign of a superior mind "is the ability to hold two opposing ideas at the same time." Do you believe this is true? And is it also true that you once said, "The only time white people tell the truth is when they keep their mouths shut"?
- A poet once wrote, "Pain is never added to pain. It multiplies." Can you tell us, in twenty-five words or less, exactly how much we all hate mathematical blackmail?
- Your son, in defining you, wrote this poem to explain one of the most significant nights in his life:

MUTUALLY ASSURED DESTRUCTION

When I was nine, my father sliced his knee
With a chain saw. But he let himself bleed
And finished cutting down one more tree
Before his boss drove him to EMERGENCY.

Late that night, stoned on morphine and beer,
My father needed my help to steer
His pickup into the woods. "Watch for deer,"
My father said. "Those things just appear

Like magic." It was an Indian summer
And we drove through warm rain and thunder,
Until we found that chain saw, lying under
The fallen pine. Then I watched, with wonder,

As my father, shotgun-rich and impulse-poor,
Blasted that chain saw dead. "What was that for?"
I asked. "Son," my father said, "here's the score.
Once a thing tastes blood, it will come for more."

- Well, first of all, as you know, you did cut your knee with a
  chain saw, but in direct contradiction to your son's poem:

  A) You immediately went to the emergency room after in-
     juring yourself.
  B) Your boss called your wife, who drove you to the emer-
     gency room.

C) You were given morphine but even you were not alcoholically stupid enough to drink alcohol while on serious narcotics.

D) You and your son did not get into the pickup that night.

E) And even if you had driven the pickup, you were not injured seriously enough to need your son's help with the pedals and/or steering wheel.

F) You never in your life used the word, *appear,* and certainly never used the phrase, like magic.

G) You also agree that Indian summer is a fairly questionable seasonal reference for an Indian poet to use.

H) What the fuck is "warm rain and thunder"? Well, everybody knows what warm rain is, but what the fuck is warm thunder?

I) You never went looking for that chain saw because it belonged to the Spokane tribe of Indians and what kind of freak would want to reclaim the chain saw that had just cut the shit out of his knee?

J) You also agree that the entire third stanza of this poem sounds like a Bruce Springsteen song and not necessarily one of the great ones.

K) And yet, "shotgun-rich and impulse-poor" is one of the greatest descriptions your son has ever written and probably redeems the entire poem.

L) You never owned a shotgun. You did own a few rifles during your lifetime, but did not own even so much as a pellet gun during the last thirty years of your life.

M) You never said, in any context, "Once a thing tastes your blood, it will come for more."

N) But you, as you read it, know that it is absolutely true and does indeed sound suspiciously like your entire life philosophy.

O) Other summations of your life philosophy include: "I'll be there before the next teardrop falls."

P) And: "If God really loved Indians, he would have made us white people."

Q) And: "Oscar Robertson should be the man on the NBA logo. They only put Jerry West on there because he's a white guy."

R) And: "A peanut butter sandwich with onions. Damn, that's the way to go."

S) And: "Why eat a pomegranate when you can eat a plain old apple. Or peach. Or orange. When it comes to fruit and vegetables, only eat the stuff you know how to grow."

T) And: "If you really want a woman to love you, then you have to dance. And if you don't want to dance, then you're going to have to work extrahard to make a woman love you forever, and you will always run the risk that she will leave you at any second for a man who knows how to tango."

U) And: "I really miss those cafeterias they use to have in Kmart. I don't know why they stopped having those. If there is a Heaven then I firmly believe it's a Kmart cafeteria."

V) And: "A father always knows what his sons are doing. For instance, boys, I knew you were sneaking that *Hustler* magazine out of my bedroom. You remember that one? Where actors who looked like Captain Kirk and

Lieutenant Uhura were screwing on the bridge of the *Enterprise*. Yeah, that one. I know you kept borrowing it. I let you borrow it. Remember this: men and pornography are like plants and sunshine. To me, porn is photosynthesis."

W) And: "Your mother is a better man than me. Mothers are almost always better men than men are."

16. Reunion

After she returned from Italy, my wife climbed into bed with me. I felt like I had not slept comfortably in years.

I said, "There was a rumor that I'd grown a tumor but I killed it with humor."

"How long have you been waiting to tell me that one?" she asked.

"Oh, probably since the first time some doctor put his fingers in my brain."

We made love. We fell asleep. But I, agitated by the steroids, woke at two, three, four, and five a.m. The bed was killing my back so I lay flat on the floor. I wasn't going to die anytime soon, at least not because of my little friend, Mr. Tumor, but that didn't make me feel any more comfortable or comforted. I felt distant from the world—from my wife and sons, from my mother and siblings—from all of my friends. I felt closer to those who've always had fingers in their brains.

And I didn't feel any closer to the world six months later when another MRI revealed that my meningioma had not grown in size or changed its shape.

"You're looking good," my doctor said. "How's your hearing?"

"I think I've got about 90 percent of it back."

"Well, then, the steroids worked. Good."

And I didn't feel any more intimate with God nine months later when one more MRI made my doctor hypothesize that my meningioma might only be more scar tissue from the hydrocephalus.

"Frankly," my doctor said. "Your brain is beautiful."

"Thank you," I said, though it was the oddest compliment I'd ever received.

I wanted to call up my father and tell him that a white man thought my brain was beautiful. But I couldn't tell him anything. He was dead. I told my wife and sons that I was okay. I told my mother and siblings. I told my friends. But none of them laughed as hard about my beautiful brain as I knew my father would have. I miss him, the drunk bastard. I would always feel closest to the man who had most disappointed me.

THE THEOLOGY OF REPTILES

We found a snake, dead in midmolt.
"It's almost like two snakes," I said.
My brother grabbed it by the head
And said, "It just needs lightning bolts."

Laughing, he jumped the creek and draped
The snake over an electric fence.
Was my brother being cruel? Yes,
But we were shocked when that damn snake

Spiraled off the wire and splayed,
Alive, on the grass, made a fist
Of itself, then, gorgeous and pissed,
Uncurled, stood on end, and swayed

For my brother, who, bemused and odd,
Had somehow become one snake's god.

CATECHISM

Why did your big brother, during one hot summer, sleep in the hall-way closet?

My mother, a Spokane Indian, kept bags of fabric scraps in that hallway closet. My brother arranged these scrap bags into shapes that approximated a mattress and pillows. My mother used these scraps to make quilts.

As an Indian, were you taught to worship the sun or the moon?

My mother was (and is) a Protestant of random varieties. My late father, a Coeur d'Alene, was a Catholic until the day that he decided to become an atheist. But it wasn't until twelve years after he decided to become an atheist that he made this information public.

MY MOTHER: "Why did you wait so long to tell us?"

MY FATHER: "I didn't want to make a quick decision."

Do you think that religious ceremony is an effective treatment for grief?

My mother once made a quilt from dozens of pairs of second- and third- and fourth-hand blue jeans that she bought at Goodwill, the Salvation Army, Value Village, and garage sales.

My late sister studied my mother's denim quilt and said, "That's a lot of pants. There's been a lot of ass in those pants. This is a blanket of asses."

If your reservation is surrounded on all sides by two rivers and a creek, doesn't that make it an island?

A Coeur d'Alene Indian holy man—on my father's side—received this vision: Three crows, luminescent and black, except for collars of white feathers, perched in a pine tree above my ancestor's camp and told him that three strangers would soon be arriving and their advice must be heeded or the Coeur d'Alene would vanish from the earth. The next day, the first Jesuits—three men in black robes with white collars—walked into a Coeur d'Alene Indian fishing camp.

Do you believe that God, in the form of his son, Jesus Christ, once walked the Earth?

Thus the Coeur d'Alene soon became, and remain, among the most Catholicized Indians in the country.

Has any member of the clergy ever given you a clear and concise explanation of this Holy Ghost business?

Therefore, nuns taught my father, as a child, to play classical piano.

Do you think that Beethoven was not actually deaf and was just having a laugh at his family's expense?

By the time I was born, my father had long since stopped play-ing piano.

ME: "Dad, what did the nuns teach you to play?"

HIM: "I don't want to talk about that shit."

After you catch a sliver from a wooden crucifix, how soon afterward will you gain superpowers?

When he was drunk, my father would sit at the kitchen table and hum an indecipherable tune while playing an imaginary keyboard.

Did your mother ever make a quilt that featured a real piano keyboard?

I have mounted my father's imaginary keyboard on my office wall.

ME: "And, here, on the wall, is my favorite work of art."

GUEST: "I don't see anything."

ME: "It's an installation piece created by my father."

GUEST: "I still can't see anything."

ME: "Exactly."

If you could only pick one word to describe your family, then what would that word be?

Honorificabilitudinitas.

Is that a real word?

Yes, Shakespeare used it. It means "The state of being able to achieve honors."

So you're stating your multisyllabic, overeducated, and pretentious belief that your family is and was in a state of being able to achieve honors?

Yep.

What kind of honors?

Whenever anybody in my family did something good, my mother would make an honor blanket. She used pieces of people's clothes and stitched in little photographs and images or important dates and names. Very ornate.

So if your mother were going to honor your family's religious history with an honor blanket, what shape would it take?

It wouldn't be an honor blanket. It would be a quilt of guilt.

Do you actually believe in God?

My mother kept scraps of God in our hallway closet. My big brother arranged these scraps of God into shapes that approximated a mattress and pillows, and slept in that closet. My mother once used these scraps of God to make an epic quilt. My late sister studied this quilt and said, "That's a lot of God. There's been a lot of God in this God. This is a blanket of God."

However, my late father, when drunk, would sit at the kitchen table and sing to an indecipherable God while playing an imaginary keyboard.

But what do you think about God?

I'm at my kitchen window, and I'm watching three crows perched on the telephone wire. I think they're talking trash about me.

ODE TO SMALL-TOWN SWEETHEARTS

O, when you are driving through a blizzard
        And your vision has been reduced—
                Has been scissored—
        Into two headlights and a noose,
How joyous to come upon the Wizard
Of Snowplows driving his glorious machine.
                Now you will survive if you ride
                        In his slipstream.
                He pushes back the fear and ice.
This is not a time for prayer, so you scream

With joy (*Snowplow! Snowplow! Snowplow! Snowplow!*)
        As he leads you into the next
                Snowed-in town.
        You are not dead! You did not wreck!
And you know a family who live here—the Browns.
They run that little diner on Main Street.
        It must be shut at this dark hour—
                Quarter past three—
        But the son, Mark, plays power
Forward for the high school, the Wolverines—

And once broke your nose with a stray elbow
　　　While playing some tough-ass defense—
　　　And you know him and call him friend.
So you park your car and trudge through the snow—
Cursing and/or blessing this fierce winter—
　　　To find Mark and his dad awake
　　　And cooking chicken-fried steaks
For a dozen other survivors and sinners.
"Dang," Mark says. "Why are you out in this stuff?"
　　　"For a girl," you say. And Mark nods.
　　　Mortals have always fought the gods
And braved epic storms for love and/or lust.
So don't be afraid to speak honestly
　　　About how you obeyed beauty's call.
　　　And though your triumph was small,
You can still sing of your teenage odyssey.

THE SENATOR'S SON

I hadn't seen my best friend in sixteen years, half of our lives ago, so I didn't recognize him when I pulled him out of the car and hit him in the face. I'd taken a few self-defense classes, so I'd learned to strike with the heel of my open hand. It's too easy to break fingers if one slams a fist against the hard bones of the head. A good student, I also remembered to stand with my feet a shoulder's width apart, for maximum balance, and to twist my hips and shoulders back before I thrust forward, for maximum leverage and striking power. And so, maximally educated, I hit my best friend and snapped his nose.

It made an astonishing noise. I imagine it could have been heard a block away. And the blood! Oh, his red glow drenched my shirt. He screamed, slumped back against his car, and slid to the ground. After that, it would have been impossible to recognize him because his face was a bloody mask. Drunk and enraged, I tried to kick him and might have beaten him unconscious or worse, but Bernard, my old college friend and drinking buddy, wrapped me in a bear hug and dragged me away.

Meanwhile, on the other side of the car, a faggot was winning his fight with Spence and Eddie, my other friends. They'd picked the wrong guy to bash. He was a talented fighter and danced, ducked, and threw mean kicks and elbows that *snap-snap-snap*ped into my friends' faces. This guy had to be one of those ultimate fighters, a mixed-martial artist.

This was in Seattle, on a dark street on Capitol Hill, the Pacific Northwest center of all things shabby, leftist, and gay. What was I, a straight Republican boy, doing on Capitol Hill? Well, it's also the home of my favorite Thai joint. I love peanut sauce and Asian beer. So my friends and I had feasted in celebration of my new junior partnership in the law firm of Robber Baron, Tax Dodger & Guilt-ridden Pro Bono. I was cash-heavy, lived in a three-bedroom condo overlooking Elliott Bay, and drove a hybrid Lexus SUV.

My father was in his first term as U.S. senator from Washington State, and he was already being talked about as a candidate for U.S. president. "I'm something different," he said to me once. "This country wants Jimmy Stewart. And I am Jimmy Stewart."

It was true. My father was handsome without being beautiful, intelligent without being pretentious, and charming without being sexual. And he was a widower, a single father who'd raised an accomplished son. My mother had died of breast cancer when I was six years old, and my father, too much in love with her memory, had never remarried. He was now as devoted and loyal to curing breast cancer as he had been to my mother.

A University of Washington Law graduate, he had begun life as the only son of a wheat farmer and his schoolteacher wife. Eagle Scout, captain of the basketball team, and homecoming king, my father was the perfect candidate. He was a city commissioner, then a state representative, and then he ran for the U.S. Senate. After decades of voting for the sons and grandsons of privilege, the state's conservatives were excited, even proud, to vote for a public school veteran, a blue-collar prince, a farmer's son, a boy with dirt in his shoes.

His best moment during his senatorial campaign was during the final debate with his Democratic rival. "My opponent keeps talking about how hard he's worked for his country, for our state. And I'm sure he has. But my grandfather and my father taught me how to be a farmer. They taught me how to plant the seed and grow the wheat that feeds our country. I worked so hard that my hands bled; look, you can still see my scars. And I promise you, my fellow Washingtonians, that I will work hard for you. And I will work hard *with* you."

My father lost liberal King County by a surprisingly close margin but kicked ass in the rest of the state and was declared senator at 9:35 P.M. on the night of the election.

Yes, my father had become Jefferson Smith and had marched into the other Washington as the first real populist in decades.

I'm not ashamed to admit that I cried a little on the night my father was elected. You've seen the photograph. It was on the cover of the *Seattle Times* and was reprinted all over the country. Everybody assumed that I was happy for my father. Overjoyed, in fact. But I was also slapped hard by grief. I desperately missed my mother, but I desperately missed my father as well. You see, he was now a U.S. senator with presidential ambitions, and that meant he belonged to everybody. I knew I'd forever lost a huge part of his energy and time and, yes, his love; I'd have to share my father with the world. I also knew I'd lost my chance to ever be anything other than an all-star politician's son.

But who wants to hear the sob story of a senator's son? The real question is this: Why the hell would I risk my reputation and future and my father's political career—the entire meaning of his life—for a street fight—for a gay bashing? I don't know, but it was high comedy.

So I laughed while that tough faggot beat Spence and Eddie into the pavement. And I laughed as Bernard dragged me toward his car, shoved me into the backseat, and slammed the door shut. Then he popped open his trunk, grabbed his tire iron, and ran back toward the fight.

I powered down the window and watched Bernard race up to that black-belt fag and threaten him with the tire iron.

"Stop this shit," Bernard yelled. "Or I'll club you."

"Why the hell are you waving that thing at me?" he screamed back. "You started it."

It was true, playground true. Spence, Eddie, Bernie, and I had started it. We'd been drunkenly ambling down the street, cussing and singing, when Spence spotted the amorous boys in their car.

"Lookit," he said. "I hate them fucking fags."

That's all it took. With banshee war cries, Spence and Eddie flung open the driver's door and dragged out the tough guy. I dragged my best friend (whom I didn't recognize) from the passenger seat and broke his nose.

And now, I was drunk in Bernard's car and he was waving a tire iron at the guy we'd assaulted.

"Come on, Spence, Eddie," Bernard said.

Bloodied and embarrassed by their beating, Spence and Eddie staggered to their feet and made their way to the car. Still waving that tire iron, Bernard also came back to me. I laughed as Spence and Eddie slid into the backseat beside me. I laughed when Bernard climbed into the driver's seat and sped us away. And I was still laughing when I looked out the rear window and saw the tough guy tending to his broken and bloody lover boy. But even as I laughed, I knew that I had committed an awful and premeditated crime: I had threatened my father's career.

Sixteen years before I dragged him out of his car and punched him in the face, my best friend Jeremy and I were smart, handsome, and ambitious young Republicans at Madison Park School in Seattle. Private and wealthy, Madison Park was filled with leftist children, parents, and faculty. Jeremy and I were the founders and leaders of the Madison Park Carnivores, a conservative club whose mission was to challenge and ridicule all things leftist. Our self-published newspaper was called *Tooth & Claw*, borrowed from the poem by Alfred Tennyson, of course, and we filled its pages with lame satire, poorly drawn cartoons, impulsive editorials, and gushing profiles of local conservative heroes, including my father, a Republican city commissioner in a Democratic city.

Looking back, I suppose I became a Republican simply because my father was a Republican. It had never occurred to me to be something different. I loved and respected my father and wanted to be exactly like him. If he'd been a plumber or a housepainter, I suppose I would have followed him into those careers. But my father's politics and vocation were only the outward manifestations of his greatness. He was my hero because of his strict moral sense. Simply put, my father kept his promises.

Jeremy, a scholarship kid and the only child of a construction worker and a housewife, was far more right wing than I was. He worried that my father, who'd enjoyed bipartisan support as city commissioner, was a leftist in conservative disguise.

"He's going to Souter us," Jeremy said. "Just you watch, he's going to Souter us in the ass."

Jeremy and I always made fun of each other's fathers. Since black kids told momma jokes, we figured we should do the opposite.

"I bet your daddy sucks David Souter's dick," Jeremy said.

Jeremy hated Supreme Court Justice David Souter, who'd been named to the court by the first President Bush. Thought to be a typical constitutional conservative, Souter had turned into a moderate maverick, a supporter of abortion rights and opponent of sodomy laws, and was widely seen by the right as a political traitor. Jeremy thought Souter should be executed for treason. Was it hyperbole? Sure, but I think he almost meant it. He was a romantic when it came to political assassination.

"When I close one eye, you look just like Lee Harvey," I said.

"I'm not Oswald," he said. "Oswald was a communist. I'm more like John Wilkes Booth."

"Come on, man, read your history. Booth killed Lincoln over slavery."

"It wasn't about slavery. It was about states' rights."

Jeremy had always enjoyed a major-league hard-on for states' rights. If it had been up to him, the United States would be fifty separate countries with fifty separate interpretations of the Constitution.

Yes, compared to Jeremy, I was more Mao than Goldwater.

It was in January of our sophomore year at Madison Park that Jeremy stole me out of class and drove me to the McDonald's in North Bend, high up in the Cascade Mountains, more than thirty miles away from our hometown of Seattle.

"What are we doing way up here?" I asked.

"Getting lunch," he said.

So we ordered hamburgers and fries from the drive-thru and ate in the car.

"I love McDonald's fries," he said.

"Yeah, they're great," I said. "But you know the best thing about them?"

"What?"

"I love that McDonald's fries are exactly the same everywhere you go. The McDonald's fries in Washington, DC, are exactly like the fries in Seattle. Heck, the McDonald's fries in Paris, France, are exactly like the fries in Seattle."

"Yeah, so what's your point?" Jeremy asked.

"Well, I think the McDonald's fries in North Bend are also exactly like the fries in Washington, DC, Paris, and Seattle. Do you agree?"

"Yeah, that seems reasonable."

"Okay, then," I said. "If all the McDonald's fries in the world are the same, why did you drive me all the way up into the mountains to buy fries we could have gotten anywhere else in the world and, most especially, in Seattle?"

"To celebrate capitalism?"

"That's funny, but it's not true," I said. "What's really going on?"

"I have something I need to tell you," Jeremy said.

"And you couldn't have told me in Seattle?"

"I didn't want anybody to hear," he said.

"Oh, nobody is going to hear anything up here," I said.

Jeremy stared out the window at Mount Si, a four-thousand-foot-tall rock left behind by one glacier or another. I usually don't pay attention to such things, but I did that day. Along with my best friend, I stared at the mountain and wondered how old it was. That's the thing: the world is old. Ancient. And humans are so temporary. But who wants to think about such things? Who wants to feel small?

"I'm getting bored," I said.

"It's beautiful up here," he said. "So green and golden."

"Yeah, whatever, Robert Frost. Now tell me why we're here."

He looked me in the eye. Stared at me for a long time. *Regarded* me.

"What?" I said, and laughed, uncomfortable as hell.

"I'm a fag," he said.

"What?" I said, and laughed.

"I'm a fag," he repeated.

"That's not funny," I said, and laughed again.

"It's kind of funny."

"Okay, yeah, it's a little funny, but it's not true."

"Yes, it is. I am a fag."

I looked into his eyes. I stared at him for a long time. I *regarded* him.

"You're telling the truth," I said.

"Yeah."

"You're a fag."

"Yeah."

"Wow."

"That's all you have to say?"

"What else am I supposed to say?" I asked.

"I was hoping you would say more than 'Wow.'"

"Well, 'Wow' is all I got."

"Damn," he said. "And I had this all planned out."

He'd been thinking about coming out to me, his unveiling, for months. At first, he'd thought about telling me while we were engaged in some overtly masculine activity, like shouting out "I'm gay!" while we were butchering a hog. Or whispering, "I'm a really good shot—for a homosexual," while we were duck hunting. Or saying, "After I'm done with Sally's vagina, it's penis and scrotum from now on," as we were screwing twin sisters in their living room.

"I'm not gay," I said.

"I know."

"I'm just saying it, so it's out there, I'm not gay. Not at all."

"Jeez, come on, I'm not interested in you like that," he said. "I'm gay, but I'm not blind."

"That's funny," I said, but I didn't laugh. I was pissed. I felt betrayed. I'd been his best friend since we were five years old, and he'd never told me how he felt. He'd never told me who he was. He'd lied to me all those years. It made me wonder what else he had lied about. After all, don't liars tell lies about everything? And sure, maybe he'd lied to protect himself from hatred and judgment. And, yes, maybe he lied because he was scared of my reaction. But a lie is a lie, right? And lying is contagious.

"You're a liar," I said.

"I know," he said, and cried.

"Ah, man," I said, "don't cry."

And then I realized how many times I'd said that to girls, to *naked* girls. I mean, don't get me wrong. I'd seen him cry before—we'd wept together at baseball games and funerals— but not in that particular context.

"I'm getting sick to my stomach," I said, which made him cry all that much harder. It felt like I was breaking up with him or something.

Maybe I wasn't being fair. But all you ever hear about are gay people's feelings. What about the feelings of the gay people's friends and family? Nobody talks about our rights. Maybe people are born gay, okay? I can deal with that, but maybe some people, like me, are born afraid of gay people. Maybe that fear is encoded in my DNA.

"I'm not gay," I said.

"Stop saying that," he said.

But I couldn't help it. I had to keep saying it. I was scared. I wondered if I was gay and didn't know it. After all, I was best friends with a fag, and he'd seen me naked. I'd seen him naked so often I could have described him to a police sketch artist. It was crazy.

"I can't take this," I said, and got out of the car. I walked over to a picnic bench and sat.

Jeremy stayed in the car and stared through the windshield at me. He wanted my love, my sweet, predictable, platonic love, the same love I'd given to him for so many years. He'd chosen me as his confessor. I was supposed to be sacred for him. But I felt like God had put a shotgun against my head and pulled the trigger. I was suddenly Hamlet, and all the uses of the world were weary, stale, flat, and unprofitable.

Jeremy stared at me. He waited for me to take action. And yes, you can condemn me for my inaction and fear. But I was only sixteen years old. Nobody had taught me how to react in such a situation. I was young and terrified and I could not move. Jeremy waited for several long minutes. I sat still, so he gave me the finger and shouted, "Fuck off!" I gave him the finger and shouted, "Fuck off!" And then Jeremy drove away.

I sat there for a few hours, bewildered. Yes, I was bewildered. When was the last time a white American male was truly bewildered or would admit to such a thing? We had taken the world from covered wagons to space shuttles in seventy-five years. After such accomplishment, how could we ever get lost in the wilderness again? How could we not invent a device to guide our souls through the darkness?

I prayed to Our Father and I called my father. And one father remained silent and the other quickly came to get me.

In that North Bend parking lot, in his staid sedan, my father trembled with anger. "What the hell are you doing up here?" he asked. He'd left a meeting with the lame-duck mayor to rescue me.

"Jeremy drove me up."

"And where is Jeremy?"

"We got in a fight. He left."

"You got into a fight?" my father asked. "What are you, a couple of girls?"

"Jeremy is a fag," I said.

"What?"

"Jeremy told me he's a fag."

"Are you homosexual?" my father asked.

I laughed.

"This is not funny," he said.

"No, it's just that word, *homosexual;* it's a goofy word."

"You haven't answered the question."

"What question?"

"Are you homosexual?"

I knew that my father still loved me, that he was still my defender. But I wondered how strong he would defend me if I were indeed gay.

"Dad, I'm not a fag. I promise."

"Okay."

"Okay."

We sat there in silence. A masculine silence. Thick and strong. Oh, I'm full of shit. We were terrified and clueless.

"Okay, Dad, what happens next?"

"I was hoping to tell you this at a better time, but I'm going to run for the State House."

"Oh, wow," I said. "Congratulations."

"I'm happy you're happy. I hated to make the decision without your input, but it had to be that way."

"I understand."

"Yes, I knew you would. And I hope you understand a few other things."

And so my father, who'd never been comfortable with my private school privilege, transferred me from Madison Park to Garfield High, a racially mixed public school in a racially mixed neighborhood.

Let my father tell you why: "The Republican Party has, for decades, silently ignored the pernicious effects of racial segregation, while simultaneously resisting any public or private efforts at integration. That time has come to an end. I am a Republican, and I love my fellow Americans, regardless of race, color, or creed. But, of course, you've heard that before. Many Republicans have issued that same kind of lofty statement while living lives entirely separate from people of other races, other classes, and other religions. Many Republicans have lied to you. And many Democrats have told you those same lies. But I will not lie, in word or deed. I have just purchased a house in the historically black Central District neighborhood of Seattle, and my son will attend Garfield High School. I am moving because I believe in action. And I am issuing a challenge to my fellow Republicans and to all Democrats, as well: Put your money, and your house, where your mouth is."

And so my father, who won the state seat with 62 percent of the vote, moved me away from Jeremy, who also left Madison Park and was homeschooled by his mother. Over the next year or so, I must have called his house twenty times. But I always hung up when he or his parents answered. And he called my private line more than twenty times, but would stay on the line and silently wait for me to speak. And then it stopped. We became rumors to each other.

Five hours after I punched Jeremy in the face, I sat alone in the living room of my childhood home in Seattle. Bernard, Spence, and Eddie were gone. I felt terrible. I prayed that I would be forgiven. No, I didn't deserve forgiveness. I prayed that I would be fairly judged. So I called the fairest man I know—my father—and told him what I had done.

The sun was rising when my father strode alone into the room and slapped me: once, twice, three times.

"Shit," he said, and stepped away.

I wiped the blood from my mouth.

"Shit," my father said once more, stepped up close to me, and slapped me again.

I was five inches taller, thirty years younger, and forty pounds heavier than my father and could have easily stopped him from hitting me. I could have hurt him. But I knew that I deserved his anger. A good son, I might have let him kill me. And, of course, I know that you doubt me. But I believe in justice. And I was a criminal who deserved punishment.

"What did you do?" my father asked.

"I don't know," I said. "I was drunk and stupid and—I don't know what happened."

"This is going to ruin everything. You've ruined me with this, this *thing*, do you understand that?"

"No, it's okay. I'll confess to it. It's all my fault. Nobody will blame you."

"Of course they'll blame me. And they *should* blame me. I'm your father."

"You're a great father."

"No, I'm not. I can't be. What kind of father could raise a son who is capable of such a thing?"

I wanted to rise up and tell my father the truth, that his son was a bloody, bawdy villain. A remorseless, treacherous, lecherous, kindless villain. But such sad and selfish talk is reserved for one's own ears. So I insulted myself with a silence that insulted my father as well.

"Don't just sit there," he said. "You can't just sit there. You have to account for yourself."

My father had always believed in truth, and in the real and vast differences between good and evil. But he'd also taught me, as he had learned, that each man is as fragile and finite as any other.

On the morning of September 11, 2001, my father prayed aloud for the victims. All day, the media worried that the body count might reach twenty or thirty thousand, so my father's prayers were the most desperate of his life. But, surprisingly, my father also prayed for the nineteen men who'd attacked us. He didn't pray for their forgiveness or redemption. No, he believed they were going to burn in a real hell. After all, what's the point of a metaphorical hell? But my father was compassionate and Christian enough to know that those nineteen men, no matter how evil their actions and corrupt their souls, could have been saved.

This is what my father taught me on that terrible day: "We are tested, all of us. We are constantly and consistently given the choice. Good or evil. Light or darkness. Love or hate. Some of those decisions are huge and tragic. Think of those nineteen men and you must curse them. But you must also curse their mothers and fathers. Curse their brothers and sisters. Curse their teachers and priests. Curse everybody who failed them. I pray for those nineteen men because I believe that some part of them, the original sliver of God that still resided in them, was calling out for guidance, for goodness and beauty. I pray for them because they chose evil and thus became evil, and I pray for them because nobody taught them how to choose goodness and become good."

Of course, my father, being a politician, could never have uttered those words in public. His supporters would not have understood the difference between empathy for a lost soul and sympathy with a terrorist's politics. Make no mistake: My father was no moral relativist. He wanted each criminal to be judged by his crimes, not by his motivations or biography.

My father refused to believe that all cultures were equal. He believed that representative democracy was a God-given gift to humans.

"I think that our perfect God will protect us in a perfect afterlife," he was fond of saying in public. "But in this highly imperfect world, we highly imperfect humans need to be protected from one another, and only a progressive republican government can guarantee any sort of protection."

In private, my father said this: "Fuck the fucking leftists and their fucking love of secularism and communism. Those bastards haven't yet figured out that the secular Hitler and the communist Stalin slaughtered millions and millions of people."

Don't get me wrong. My father knew that the world was complicated and unpredictable—and that only God knew the ultimate truth—but he also knew that each citizen of that world was ultimately responsible for his actions. My father staked his political career, his entire life, on one basic principle: An unpredictable world demands a predictable moral code.

"Son," my father said to me many a time in the years after September 11, "a thief should be judged by the theft. A rapist should be judged by the rape. A murderer should be judged by the murder. A terrorist should be judged by the terror."

And so I sat, a man capable of inexplicable violence against an innocent, eager to be judged by my God and by my father. I wanted to account and be held accountable.

"I'm sorry," I said. "I shouldn't have attacked those men. I shouldn't have walked away from the scene. At least, I should have gone back to the scene. I should go back now and turn myself in to the police."

"But you're not telling me why you did it," my father said. "Can you tell me that? Why did you do it?"

I searched my soul for an answer and could not find one. I could not make sense of it. But if I'd known that it was Jeremy I'd assaulted, I could have spoken about Cain and Abel and let my father determine the moral of the story.

"Spence and Eddie—"

"No," my father interrupted. "This is not about them. This is about you."

"Okay," I said. "I'm really confused here, Dad. I'm trying to do the right thing. And I need you to help me. Tell me what the right thing is. Tell me what I'm supposed to do."

And so my father told me what he had learned from confidential sources. The gay men had reported the assault but, obviously shocked and confused, had provided conflicting descriptions of Spence, Eddie, and Bernard and no description of me other than "white male, twenties to thirties, five-eight to six feet, one-eighty to two hundred pounds." In other words, I could have been almost any Caucasian guy in Seattle. The victims didn't catch the license plate of the suspects' car and could only describe it as a "dark four-door." There were no other witnesses to the assault as of yet. Most curious, the victims disagreed on whether or not the perpetrators brandished guns.

"What do the police think?" I asked.

"They think the victims are hiding something," my father said.

"They're just scared and freaked out."

"No. I agree with the police. I think they're hiding something."

"No, they're not hiding anything, Dad. They're just confused. I'd be confused if somebody attacked me like that."

"No, they're hiding the fact that they started the fight and they don't want the police to know it."

I was shocked. Was this really my father or his lying twin? Was I talking to my father or his murderous brother?

"Listen," he said. "I don't think the police really have anything to go on. And I don't think they're going to pursue this much further. But we're going to monitor the investigation very closely. And we're going to be preemptive if we sense any real danger."

"What are you talking about? Are you going to hurt them?"

More enraged than ever before, my father grabbed me by the shirt. "Don't you say such things. Don't you dare! This is the United States of America, not some third world shit heap! I am not in the business of intimidation or violence. I am not in the business of murder."

It was true. My father believed in life, the sacred spark of humans, more strongly than any other man I'd ever known. As a Republican, he was predictably antiabortion, but he was also against capital punishment. His famous speech: "It is the business of man to judge and punish on this mortal Earth; but it is the business of God to give and take away life. I believe that abortion is a great evil, but it is just as evil to abandon any child to the vagaries of economics. I believe it is evil to murder another human being, but it is just as evil for a government to kill its citizens based on the vagaries of justice."

Yes, this was the man I had accused of conspiracy. I had insulted my father. I'd questioned his honor. I'd deemed him capable of murder. He was right to shake me.

"I'm sorry," I said. "I'm sorry. I'm just confused. Help me. Please, Daddy, help me. I love you. Please, please help me."

And so he held me while I wept.

"I love you, son," he said. "But you have to listen to me. You have to understand. I know that you were wrong to do what you did. It was a mortal sin. You sinned against God, against those men, and against me. And you should pay for those sins."

My good father wanted me to be a good man.

"But it's not that easy," my father said. "If you turn yourself in to the police, I will also pay for your sins. And I know I should pay for your sins because I am your father, and I have obviously failed to raise you well. But I will also pay for your sins as a U.S. senator, so our state and country will also pay for them. A scandal like this will ruin my career. It will ruin our party. And it will ruin our country. And though I know I will be judged harshly by God, I can't let you tell the truth."

My father wanted me to lie. No, he was forcing me to lie.

"William, Willy," he said. "If we begin to suspect that you might be implicated in this, we're going to go on the offensive. We're going to kill their reputations."

If it is true that children pay for the sins of their fathers, is it also true that fathers pay for the sins of their children?

Three days later, I returned to my condominium in downtown Seattle and found a message waiting on my voice mail.

"Hey, William, it's—um, me, Jeremy. You really need to call me."

And so I called Jeremy and agreed to meet him at his house in Magnolia, an upper-class neighborhood of Seattle. It was a small but lovely house, painted blue and chocolate.

I rang the doorbell. Jeremy answered. His face and nose were swollen purple, yellow, and black; his eyes were bloodshot and tear-filled.

"It was you," I said, suddenly caught in an inferno of shame.

"Of course it was me. Get your ass in here."

Inside, we sat in his study, a modernist room decorated with beautiful and useless furniture. What good is a filing cabinet that can only hold an inch of paperwork?

"I'm so sorry, Jeremy," I said. "I didn't know it was you."

"Oh, so I'm supposed to be happy about that? Things would be okay if you'd beaten the shit out of a fag you didn't know?"

"That's not what I meant."

"Okay, then, what did you mean?"

"I was wrong to do what I did. Completely wrong."

"Yes, you were," he said.

He was smiling. I recognized that smile. Jeremy was giving me shit. Was he going to torture me before he killed me?

"Why didn't you tell the police it was me?" I asked.

"Because the police don't give a shit about fags."

"But we assaulted you. We could have killed you."

"Doubtful. James had already kicked the crap out of your friends. And he would have kicked the crap out of you and the guy with the tire iron. Let's just call it a split decision."

"You didn't tell James it was me, did you?"

"No, of course not. I told the police a completely different story than James did. And I was the one with the broken face, so they believed me."

"But what about James? What's he going to do?"

"Oh, who cares? I barely knew him."

"But it was a hate crime."

"Aren't all crimes, by definition, hate crimes? I mean, people don't rob banks because they love tellers."

"I don't understand you. Why haven't you gone public with this? You could destroy my father. And me."

Jeremy sighed.

"Oh, William," he said. "You're still such an adolescent. And so romantic. I haven't turned you in because I'm a Republican, a good one, and I think your father is the finest senator we've ever had. I used to think he was a closet Democrat. But he's become something special. This kind of shit would completely fuck his chance at the presidency."

Jesus, was this guy more a son to my father than I was?

"And, okay, maybe I'm a romantic, too," Jeremy said. "I didn't turn you in because we were best friends and because I still consider you my best friend."

"But my father hates gay people."

"It's more complicated than that."

And so Jeremy explained to me that his sexual preference had nothing to do with his political beliefs.

"Hey," he said. "I don't expect to be judged negatively for my fuck buddies. But I don't want to be judged positively, either. It's just sex. It's not like it's some specialized skill or something. Hell, right now, in this house, one hundred thousand bugs are fucking away. In this city, millions of bugs are fucking at this very moment. And, hey, probably ten thousand humans—and registered voters—are fucking somewhere in this city. Four or five of them might even be married."

"So what's your point?"

"Anybody who thinks that sex somehow relates to the national debt or terrorism or poverty or crime or moral values or any kind of politics is just an idiot."

"Damn, Jeremy, you've gotten hard."

"That's what all the boys say."

"And what does James say? What if he goes to the press? What if he sees my face in the newspapers or on TV and recognizes me?"

"James is a little fag coffee barista from Bumfuck, Idaho. Nobody cares what he has to say. Little James could deliver a Martian directly to the White House and people would think it was a green poodle with funny ears."

I wondered if I'd completely scrambled Jeremy's brains when I punched him in the head.

"Will you listen to me?" I said. "My father will destroy your life if he feels threatened."

"Did you know your father called my father that day up in North Bend?" Jeremy asked.

"What day?" I asked. But I knew.

"Don't be obtuse. After I told you I was gay, you told your father, and your father told my father. And my father beat the shit out of me."

"You're lying," I said. But I knew he wasn't.

"You think my face looks bad now? Oh, man, my dad broke my cheekbone. Broke my arm. Broke my leg. A hairline fracture of the skull. A severe concussion. I saw double for two months."

"How come you didn't go to the police?"

"Oh, my dad took me to the police. Said a gang of kids did it to me. Hoodlums, he called them."

"How come you didn't tell the police the truth?"

"Because my dad said he'd kill my mom if I told the truth."

"I don't think I believe any of this."

"You can believe what you want. I know what happened. My father beat the shit out of me because he was ashamed of me. And I let him because I was ashamed of me. And because I loved my mom."

I stared at him. Could he possibly be telling the truth? Are there truths as horrible as this one? In abandoning him when he was sixteen, did I doom him to a life with a violent father and a beaten mother?

"But you know the best thing about all of this?" he asked.

I couldn't believe there'd be any good in this story.

"When my father was lying in his hospital bed, he asked for me," Jeremy said. "Think about it. My father was dying of cancer. And he called for me. He needed me to forgive him. And you know what?"

"What?" I asked, though I didn't want to know.

"I went into his room, hugged him and told him I forgave him and I loved him, and we cried and then he died."

"I can't believe any of this."

"It's all true."

"You forgave your father?" I asked.

"Yeah," Jeremy said. "It really made me wish I was Roman or Greek, you know? A classical Greek god would have killed his lying, cheating father and *then* given him forgiveness. And a classical Greek god would have better abs, too. That's what Greek gods are all about, you know? Patricide and low body fat."

How could anybody be capable of that much forgiveness? I was reminded of the black man, the convicted rapist, who'd quietly proclaimed his innocence all during his thirty years in prison. After he was exonerated by DNA evidence and finally freed, that black man completely forgave the white woman who'd identified him as her rapist. He said he forgave her because it would do him no good to carry that much anger in his heart. I often wonder if that man was Jesus come back.

"The thing is, Willy," Jeremy said, "you've always been such a moral guy. Six years old, and you made sure that everybody got equal time on the swings, on the teeter-totter, on the baseball field. Even the losers. And you learned that from your father."

"My father is a great man," I said, but I wasn't sure I believed it. I had to believe it, though, or my foundations would collapse.

"No," Jeremy said. "Your father has great ideas, but he's an ordinary man, just like all of us. No, your father is more of an asshole than usual. He likes to hit people."

"He's only hit me a couple of times."

"That you can remember."

"What does that mean?"

"We wouldn't practice denial if it didn't work."

"Fuck you," I said.

"Oh, you're scary. What are you going to do, punch me in the face?"

We laughed.

"It comes down to this," Jeremy said. "You can't be a great father and a great politician at the same time. Impossible. Can't be a great father and a great writer, either. Just ask Hemingway's kids."

"I prefer Faulkner."

"Yeah, there's another candidate for Father of the Year."

"Okay, okay, writers are bad dads. What's your point?"

"Your father is great because of his ideas. And those great ideas will make him a great president."

"Why do you believe in him so much?"

"It's about sacrifice. Listen, I am a wealthy American male. I can't campaign for something as silly and fractured as gay marriage when there are millions of Muslim women who can't even show their ankles. Your daddy knows that. Everybody knows it."

"I don't know anything."

"I hate to sound like a campaign worker or something, but listen to me. I believe in him so much that I'll pay ten bucks for a gallon of gas. I believe in him so much that I'm going to let you go free."

I wondered if Jeremy had been beaten so often that it had destroyed his spirit. Had he lost the ability to defend himself? How many times could he forgive the men who had bloodied and broken him? Is there a finite amount of forgiveness in the world? Was there a point after which forgiveness, even the most divinely inspired, is simply the act of a coward? Or has forgiveness always been used as political capital?

"Jeremy," I asked, "what am I supposed to do with all this information?"

"That's up to you, sweetheart."

Oh, there are more things in heaven and earth than can be explained by *Meet the Press*.

Jeremy and I haven't talked since that day. We agreed that our friendship was best left abandoned in the past. My crime against him was also left in the past. As expected, the police did not pursue the case, and it was soon filed away. There was never any need to invent a story.

I cannot tell you what happened to James, or to Eddie and Spence, or to Bernard. We who shared the most important moment of our lives no longer have any part in the lives of the others. It happens that way. I imagine that someday one of them might try to tell the whole story. And I imagine nobody would believe them. Who would believe any of them? Or me? Has a liar ever told the truth?

As for my father, he lost his reelection bid and retired to the relatively sad life of an ex-senator. He plays golf three times a week. State leaders beg for his advice.

My father and I have never again discussed that horrible night. We have no need or right to judge each other for sins that might have already doomed us to a fiery afterlife. Instead, we both silently forgave each other, and separately and loudly pray to God for his forgiveness. I'll let you know how that works out.

ANOTHER PROCLAMATION

When
Lincoln
Delivered
The
Emancipation
Proclamation,
Who
Knew

that, one year earlier, in 1862, he'd signed and approved the
order for the largest public execution in United States history?
Who did they execute? "Mulatto, mixed-bloods, and Indians."
Why did they execute them? "For uprisings against the State
and her citizens." Where did they execute them? Mankato,
Minnesota. How did they execute them? Well, Abraham Lincoln thought it was good

And
Just
To
Hang
Thirty-eight
Sioux

simultaneously. Yes, in front of a large and cheering crowd, thirty-eight Indians dropped to their deaths. Yes, thirty-eight necks snapped. But before they died, thirty-eight Indians sang their death songs. Can you imagine the cacophony of thirty-eight different death songs? But wait, one Indian was pardoned at the last minute, so only thirty-seven Indians had to sing their death songs. But, O, O, O, O, can you imagine the cacophony of that one survivor's mourning song? If he taught you the words, do you think you would sing along?

Invisible Dog on a Leash

1.

In 1973, my father and I saw *Enter the Dragon*, the greatest martial arts movie of all time. I loved Bruce Lee. I wanted to be Bruce Lee. Afterward, as we walked to our car, I threw punches and kicks at the air.

"Hey, Dad," I asked, "is Bruce Lee the toughest guy in the world?"

My father said, "No way. There are five guys in Spokane who could probably kick Bruce Lee's ass."

"Really? You mean in a fair fistfight and everything?"

"Who said anything about fair? And who'd want to throw punches with Bruce Lee? I'm not talking about fists. I'm saying there are at least five guys in Spokane who, if they even saw Bruce Lee, they'd walk up to him and just sucker punch him with a baseball bat or a two-by-four or something."

"That's not right."

"You didn't ask me about right. You asked me about tough."

"Are you tougher than Bruce Lee?"

"Well, I'm tough in some ways, I guess. But I'm not the kind of guy who will knock somebody in the head with a baseball bat. I'm not going to do that to Bruce Lee. But let me tell you, there are more than five guys in Spokane who would do that. As I'm thinking more and more about it, I'm thinking there are probably fifty crazy guys who'd sneak up behind Bruce Lee at a restaurant and just knock him out with a big frying pan or something."

"Okay, Dad, that's enough."

"And I haven't even talked about prison dudes. Shoot, every other guy in prison would be happy to sucker punch Bruce Lee. They'd wait in a dark corner for a week, just waiting to ambush Bruce Lee with a chain saw or something. Man, those prison guys aren't going to mess around with a Jeet Kune Do guy like Bruce Lee. No way. Those prison dudes would build a catapult and fling giant boulders at Bruce Lee."

"Okay, Dad, I believe you. I've heard enough. Stop it, Dad, stop it!"

"Okay, Okay, I'm sorry. I'm just telling you the truth."

2.

On TV, Uri Geller was bending spoons
With just his mind. "Wow," I said. "That's so cool."

Then, three days later, as I browsed through Rick's
Pawn Shop, I picked up a book of magic tricks

And learned how to bend spoons almost as well.
I called my act URI GELLER IS GOING TO HELL.

3.

At Expo '74, in Spokane, I saw my first invisible dog on a leash. A hilarious and agile Chinese man was selling them.

"My dog is fast," he said. And his little pet, in its leash and harness, dragged him across the grass. I thought it was real magic. I didn't know it was just an illusion. I didn't know that thick and flexible wires had been threaded through the leash and harness and then shaped to look like a dog—an invisible dog. In fact, I didn't discover the truth until two years later at our tribe's powwow, when a felonious-looking white man tried to sell me an invisible dog with a broken leash. Without a taut leash, that invisible dog didn't move or dance in its harness. The magic was gone. I was an emotional kid, so I started to cry, and the felonious dude said, "Shit, kid, take it, I found it in the garbage anyway."

4.

In '76, I also saw the remake of *King Kong*. It was terrible. Even my father, who loved the worst drive-in exploitation crap, said, "It's Kong, man. What went so wrong?" But that does remind me of a drive-in flick whose name I can't recall. It's about a herd of Sasquatch who sneak into a biker gang's house and kidnap all of the biker women. Later, the biker gang puts spiked wheels on their rods, roars into the woods, somehow finds the Sasquatch, and battles for the women. As the Sasquatch fight and fall and pretend to die, two or three of them lose their costume heads. Their furry masks just go sailing but the actors playing Sasquatch, and the other actors, and the director, and the writer, and the producers, and God just keep on going as if it didn't matter. And I suppose, for the sake of budget, it *didn't* matter, but I stood on the top of our van and shouted, "It's not real. It's not real. It's not real. It's not real!" And some politically aware but unseen dude shouted from out of the dark, "Okay, Little Crazy Horse, we know it's not real, so get your ass back in your van."

5.

Speaking of Sasquatch, I met the love of my life in 1979, in Redding, California, the heart of Bigfoot Country. Okay, she wasn't the love of my life, she just happened to be the first world-class beauty I'd ever seen. Honestly. She could have been on the cover of *Glamour* magazine. But she was just a teenage girl from Redding, California, which, like I said, was the heart of Bigfoot Country. And I was obsessed with Bigfoot, with the real Sasquatch, not the fake biker-gang-fighting and biker-chick-kidnapping type. So, as this gorgeous girl asked me what I wanted (my family had stopped to eat at some fast-food joint on our way to Disneyland), I said, "Isn't it cool to live in Bigfoot Country? In the heart of Bigfoot Country. In the heart of the heart of Bigfoot Country."

"Oh," she said. "That stuff ain't real. It's my two uncles—Little Jim and Big Jim—who make all those footprints with these big wooden feet they carved out and tie up on their boots."

"What?"

"Yeah. If you've ever seen that movie *Planet of the Apes*, you've seen my uncles, because they played gorillas."

"Are you kidding?"

"No, my uncles used to work at the San Francisco Zoo when they were in college. They helped feed the gorillas and monkeys and chimps and stuff. So they really learned how to walk around like apes. But those Hollywood people didn't appreciate them, you know? Didn't pay them hardly anything for being in that first *Planet* movie. So my uncles didn't work on any of the sequels."

"I can't believe what I'm hearing."

"Well, it's all true. You can even go visit my uncles if you want. They've got a bunch of those fake Bigfoot feet you can buy. And if you tell them I sent you over, they'll even show you their Bigfoot costumes."

"They have costumes?"

"Yeah, and you will not believe how much those costumes look like a real Bigfoot. It was Big Jim who was playing Bigfoot in that famous movie. You've seen that one, right? The one where Bigfoot is walking across the riverbed? Yeah, whenever I see that video on TV, I scream, "Hey, Uncle Big Jim!" Anyway, I have to remember my job. What do you want to eat, little man?"

"A corn dog, I guess."

Home of the Braves

When my female friends are left
By horrid spouses and lovers,
I commiserate. I send gifts—
Powwow songs and poems—and wonder

Why my gorgeous friends cannot find
Someone who knows them as I do.
Is the whole world deaf and blind?
I tell my friends, "I'd marry you

Tomorrow." I think I'm engaged
To thirty-six women, my harem:
Platonic, bookish, and enraged.
I love them! But it would scare them—

No, of course, they already know
That I can be just one more boy,
A toy warrior who explodes
Into silence and warpaths with joy.

THE BALLAD OF
PAUL NONETHELESS

In Chicago's O'Hare Airport, walking east on a moving sidewalk, Paul saw a beautiful woman walking west. She'd pulled her hair back into a messy ponytail, and her blue jeans were dark-rinsed boot-cut, and her white T-shirt was a size too small, and her pale arms were muscular. And—ah, she wore a pair of glorious red shoes. Pumas. Paul knew those shoes. He'd seen them in an ad in a fashion magazine, or maybe on an Internet site, and fallen in love with them. Allegedly an athletic shoe, the red Pumas were really a thing of beauty. On any woman, they'd be lovely; on this woman, they were glorious. Who knew that Paul would someday see those shoes on a woman's feet and feel compelled to pursue her?

Paul wanted to shout out, *I love your Pumas!* He wanted to orate it with all the profundity and passion of a Shakespearean couplet, but that seemed too eccentric and desperate and—well, literate. He wanted the woman to know he was instantly but ordinarily attracted to her, so he smiled and waved instead. But bored with her beauty, or more likely bored with the men who noticed her beauty, she ignored Paul and rolled her baggage on toward the taxi or parking shuttle or town car.

"'She's gone, she's gone.'" Paul sang the chorus of that Hall & Oates song. He sang without irony, for he was a twenty-first-century American who'd been taught to mourn his small and large losses by singing Top 40 hits.

There was a rule book: When a man is rebuffed by a beautiful stranger he must sing blue-eyed soul; when a man is drunk with the loneliness of being a frequent flyer he must sing Mississippi Delta blues; when a man wants revenge he must whistle the sound track of *The Good, the Bad, and the Ugly*. When a man's father and mother die within three months of each other, he must sing Rodgers and Hammerstein: "Oklahoma! Oklahoma Okay!"

Despite all the talk of diversity and division—of red and blue states, of black and white and brown people, of rich and poor, gay and straight—Paul believed that Americans were shockingly similar. How can we be so different, thought Paul, if we all know the lyrics to the same one thousand songs? Paul knew the same lyrics as any random guy from Mobile, Alabama, or woman from Orono, Maine. Hell, Paul had memorized, without effort or ever purchasing or downloading one of their CDs—or even one of their songs—the complete works of Garth Brooks, Neil Diamond, and AC/DC. And if words and music can wind their way into and around our DNA strands—and Paul believed they could—wouldn't American pop music be passed from generation to generation as easily as blue eyes or baldness? Hadn't pop music created a new and invisible organ, a pituitary gland of the soul, in the American body? Or were these lies and exaggerations? Could one honestly say that Elvis is a more important figure in American history than Einstein? Could one posit that Aretha Franklin's version of "Respect" was more kinetic and relevant to American life than Dwight D. Eisenhower's 1961 speech that warned us about the dangers of a military-industrial complex? Could a reasonable person think that Madonna's "Like a Prayer" was as integral and universal to everyday life as the fork or wheel? Paul believed all these heresies about pop music but would never say them aloud for fear of being viewed as a less-than-serious person.

Or wait, maybe Paul wasn't a serious person. Maybe he was an utterly contemporary and callow human being. Maybe he was an American ironic. Maybe he was obsessed with pop music because it so perfectly reflected his current desires. And yet, Paul sold secondhand clothes for a living. He owned five vintage clothing stores in the Pacific Northwest and was currently wearing a gray tweed three-piece suit once owned by Gene Kelly. So Paul was certainly not addicted to the present day. On the contrary, Paul believed that the present, past, and future were all happening simultaneously, and that any era's pop culture was *his* pop culture. And sure, pop culture could be crass and manipulative, and sometimes evil, but it could also be magical and redemptive.

Take Irving Berlin, for example. He was born Israel Baline in Russia in 1888, emigrated with his family in 1893 to the United States, and would eventually write dozens, if not hundreds, of classic tunes, including, most famously, "Alexander's Ragtime Band." Yes, it was a Russian Jew who wrote the American love song that suggested we better hurry and meander at the same time. Can a person simultaneously hurry and meander? Yes, in the United States a romantic is, by definition, a person filled with those contradictions. And, the romantic American is in love with his contradictions. And the most romantic Americans (see Walt Whitman) want to have contradictory sex. Walt Whitman would have wanted to have sex with Irving Berlin. Paul loved Irving Berlin and Walt Whitman. He loved the thought of their sexual union. And most of all, Paul loved the fact that Irving Berlin had lived a long and glorious life and died in 1989, only sixteen years earlier.

Yes, Irving Berlin was still alive in 1989. It's quite possible that Irving Berlin voted for Michael Dukakis for United States president. How can you not love a country and a culture where that kind of beautiful insanity can flourish? But wait— did any of this really matter anyway? Was it just the musical trivia of a trivial man in a trivial country? And beyond all that, why was Paul compelled to defend his obsessions? Why was he forced to define and self-define? After all, one doesn't choose his culture nearly as much as one trips and falls into it.

Splat! Paul was a forty-year-old man from Seattle, Washington, who lived only ten minutes from the house where Kurt Cobain shotgunned himself, and only fifteen minutes from the stretch of Jackson Street where Ray Charles and Quincy Jones began their careers in bygone jazz clubs. *Splat!* Paul's office, and the headquarters of his small used-clothes empire, was down the street from a life-size statue of Jimi Hendrix ripping an all-weather solo. *Splat!* Paul bought his morning coffee at the same independent joint where a dozen of Courtney Love's bounced checks decorated the walls.

Paul believed American greatness and the ghosts of that greatness surrounded him. But who could publicly express such a belief and not be ridiculed as a patriotic fool? Paul believed in his fellow Americans, in their extraordinary decency, in their awesome ability to transcend religion, race, and class, but what leftist could state such things and ever hope to get laid by any other lefty? And yet Paul was the perfect example of American possibility: He made a great living (nearly $325,000 the previous tax year) by selling secondhand clothes.

For God's sake, Paul was flying to Durham, North Carolina, for a denim auction. A Baptist minister had found one hundred pairs of vintage Levi's (including one pair dating back to the nineteenth century that was likely to fetch $25,000 or more!) in his father's attic, and was selling them to help raise money for the construction of a new church. Blue jeans for God! Blue jeans for Jesus! Blue Jeans for the Holy Ghost!

Used clothes for sale! Used clothes for sale! That was Paul's capitalistic war cry. That was his mating song.

Thus unhinged and aroused, Paul turned around and ran against the moving sidewalk. He chased after the beautiful woman—in her gorgeous red Pumas—who had rebuffed him. He wanted to tell her everything that he believed about his country. No, he just wanted to tell her that music—pop music— was the most important thing in the world. He would show her the top twenty-five songs played on his iPod, and she'd have sex with him in the taxi or parking shuttle or town car.

And there she was, on the escalator above him, with her perfect jeans and powerful yoga thighs. Paul could hear her denim singing friction ballads across her skin. Paul couldn't remember the last time he'd had sex with a woman who wore red shoes. Paul dreamed of taking them off and taking a deep whiff. Ha! He'd instantly developed a foot fetish. He wanted to smell this woman's feet. Yes, that was the crazy desire in his brain and his crotch when he ran off the escalator and caught the woman outside of the security exit.

"Excuse me, I'm sorry, hello," Paul said.

She stared at him. She studied his face, wondering if she knew him, or if he was a gypsy cab driver, or if he was a creep.

"I saw you back there on the moving sidewalk," Paul said.

Wow, that was a stupid thing to say. That meant nothing. No, that meant Paul had noticed the lovely shapes of her green eyes, breasts, and ass—their mystical geometry—and that made him as ordinary, if slightly more mathematical, as any other man in the airport. He needed to say something extraordinary, something poetic, in order to make her see that he was capable of creating, well, extraordinary poetry. Could he talk about her shoes? Was that a convincing way to begin this relationship? Or maybe he could tell her that Irving Berlin's real name was Israel.

"I mean," Paul said, "well, I wanted to—well, the thing is, I saw you—no, I mean—well, I did see you, but it wasn't sight that made me chase after you, you know? I mean—it wasn't really any of my five senses that did it. It was something beyond that. You exist beyond the senses; I just know that without really knowing it, you know?"

She smiled. The teeth were a little crowded. The lines around her eyes were new. She was short, a little over five feet tall, and, ah, she wore those spectacular red shoes. If this didn't work out, Paul was going to run home and buy the DVD version of that movie about the ballerina's red dance slippers. Or was he thinking of the movie about the kid who lost his red balloon? Somewhere there must be a movie about a ballerina who ties her dance shoes to a balloon and watches them float away. *Jesus*, Paul said to himself. *Focus, focus.*

"You have a beautiful smile," Paul said to the stranger. "And if your name is Sara, I'm going to lose my mind."

"My name isn't Sara," she said. "Why would you think my name is Sara?"

"You know, great smile, name is Sara. 'Sara Smile'? The song by Hall and Oates."

"Oh, yeah, that's a good one."

"You've made me think of two Hall and Oates songs in, like, five minutes. I think that's a sign. Of what, I don't know, but a sign nonetheless."

"I think that's the first time I've ever heard a man say *nonetheless* in normal conversation."

Was she mocking him? Yes, she was. Was that a positive step in their relationship? Did it imply a certain familiarity or the desire for a certain familiarity? And, by the way, when exactly had he become the kind of man who uses *nonetheless* in everyday conversation?

"Listen," Paul said to the beautiful stranger. "I don't know you. And you don't know me. But I want to talk to you—and listen to you; that's even more important—I want to talk and listen to you for a few hours. I want to share stories. That's it. That's it exactly. I think you have important stories to tell. Stories I need to hear."

She laughed and shook her head. Did he amuse her? Or bemuse her? There was an important difference: Women sometimes slept with bemusing men, but they usually *married* amusing men.

"So, listen," Paul said. "I am perfectly willing to miss my flight and have coffee with you right here in the airport—and if that makes you feel vulnerable, just remember there are dozens of heavily armed security guards all around us—so, please, if you're inclined to spend some time with a complete but devastatingly handsome stranger, I would love your company."

"Well," she said. "You *are* cute. And I like your suit."

"It used to belong to Gene Kelly. He wore it in one of his movies."

"*Singin' in the Rain?*"

"No, one of the bad ones. When people talk about the golden age of Hollywood musicals, they don't realize that almost all of them were bad."

"Are you a musician?"

"Uh, no, I sell used clothes. Vintage clothes. But only the beautiful stuff, you know?"

"Like your suit."

"Yes, like my suit."

"Sounds like a cool job."

"It *is* a cool job. I have, like, one of the coolest lives ever. You should know that."

"I'm sure you are a very cool individual. But I'm married, and my husband is waiting for me at baggage claim."

"I don't want this to be a comment on the institution of marriage itself, which I believe in, but I want you to know that your marriage, while great for your husband and you, is an absolute tragedy for me. I'm talking Greek tragedy. I'm talking mothers-killing-their-children level of tragedy. If you listened to my heart, you'd hear that it just keeps beating *Medea, Medea, Medea*. And yes, I know the rhythm is off on that. Makes me sound like I have a heart murmur."

She laughed. He'd made her laugh three or four times since they'd met. He'd turned the avenging and murderous Medea into a sexy punch line. How many men could do that?

"Hey," she said. "Thank you for the—uh—attention. You've made my day. Really. But I must go. I'll see you in the next life."

She turned to leave, but then she paused—O, *che sarà!*—leaned in close to Paul, and gave him a soft kiss on the cheek. Then she laughed again and walked away. No, it wasn't just a walk. It was a magical act of transportation. Delirious, Paul watched her leave. He marveled at the gifts of strangers, at the way in which a five-minute relationship can be as gratifying and complete (and sexless!) as a thirteen-year marriage. Then he made his way back through security and to his gate, caught his flight to North Carolina, and bought a pair of 1962 Levi's for $1,250.

Of course, Paul was a liar, a cheater, and a thief. He'd pursued the beautiful airport stranger without giving much thought to his own marriage. And sure, he was separated, and his wife and three teenage daughters were living in the family home while Paul lived in a one-bedroom on Capitol Hill, but he was still married and wanted to remain married. He loved his wife, didn't he? Well, of course he did. She was lovely (was more than that, really) and smart and funny and all those things an attractive human being is supposed to be, and she in turn thought Paul was a lovely, smart, funny, and attractive human being. They had built a marriage based on their shared love of sixties soul music on vinyl—and vintage clothes, of course. Or perhaps

Paul had built this life and his wife had followed along. In any case, they were happy, extraordinarily happy, right? Jesus, it was easy to stay happy in a first-world democracy. What kind of madman would stay that long in an unhappy marriage, especially in an age when people divorced so easily? Yes, Paul loved his wife; he was in love with her. He was sure he could pass a lie-detector test on that one. And he loved his three daughters. He was more sure about that.

But if he was so happy, if he was so in love with his wife and daughters, why was he separated from them? Sadly, it was all about sex—or, rather, the lack of sex. Simply and crudely stated, Paul had lost the desire to fuck his wife. How had that happened? Paul didn't know, exactly. And he couldn't talk to anybody about it. How could he tell his friends, his circle of men, that he had no interest in sleeping with the sexiest woman any of them had ever met? She was so beautiful that she intimidated many of his friends. His best friend, Jacob, had once drunkenly confessed that he still couldn't look her directly in the eyes.

"I've known her, what, almost twenty years?" Jacob had said. "And I still have to look at her out of the corner of my eye. I'm the godfather to your daughters, and I have to talk to their mother with my sideways vision. You remember the time we all got drunk and naked in my hot tub? She was so amazing, so perfect, that I had to run around the corner and throw up. Your wife was so beautiful she made me sick. I hope you know how lucky you are, you lucky bastard."

Yes, Paul knew he was lucky: He had a great job, great daughters, and a great wife that he didn't want to fuck. And so he, the lucky bastard, had sex with every other possible partner. During his marriage, Paul had had sex with eight other women: two employees, three ex-girlfriends, two of his friends' wives, and a woman with one of the largest used-clothing stores on eBay.

After that last affair, a clumsy and incomplete coupling in a San Francisco apartment crowded with vintage sundresses and UPS boxes, Paul had confessed to his wife. Oh, no, he didn't confess to all his infidelities. That would have been too much. It would have been cruel. Instead, he only admitted to the one but carefully inserted details of the other seven, so that his confession would be at least fractionally honest. His wife had listened silently, packed him a bag, and kicked him out of the house. What was the last thing she'd said? "I can't believe you fucked somebody from eBay."

And so, for a year now, Paul had lived apart from his family. And had been working hard to win back their love. He'd been chaste while recourting his wife. But he was quite sure that she doubted his newly found fidelity—he traveled too damn much ever to be thought of as a good candidate for stability—and he'd heard from his daughters that a couple of men, handsome strangers, had come calling on his wife. He couldn't sleep some nights when he thought about other men's hands and cocks and mouths touching his wife. How strange, Paul thought, to be jealous of other men's lust for the woman who had only wanted, and had lost, her husband's lust. And stranger and more contradictory, Paul vanquished his jealousy by furiously masturbating while fantasizing about his dream wife fucking dream men. Feeling like a fool, but hard anyway, Paul stroked as other men—nightmares—pushed into his wife. And when those vision men came hard, Paul also came hard. Everybody was arched and twisted. And oh, Paul was afraid—terrified—of how good it felt. What oath, what marital vow, did he break by imagining his wife's infidelity? None, he supposed, but he felt primitive, like the first ape that fell from the high trees and, upon landing, decided to live upright, use tools, and evolve. *Dear wife,* Paul wanted to say, *I'm quite sure that you will despise me for these thoughts, and I respect your need to keep our lives private, to relock the doors of our home, but I, primal and vain, still need to boast about my fears and sins. Inside my cave, I build fires to scare away the ghosts and keep the local predators at bay, or perhaps I build fires to attract hungry carnivores. Could I be that dumb? Dear wife, watch me celebrate what I lack. I am as opposable as my thumbs.* Ah, Paul thought, who cares about the color of a man's skin when his true identity is much deeper—subterranean—and far more diverse and disturbing than the ethnicity of his mother and father? And yet, nobody had ever argued for the civil rights of contradictory masturbators. "Chances are," Paul often sang to himself while thinking of his marriage. "Chances are." And he was singing that song in a Los Angeles International Airport bookstore—on his way home from the largest flea market in Southern California—when he saw the beautiful stranger who had rebuffed him three months earlier at O'Hare.

"Hey," he said. "It's Sara Smile."

She looked up from the book she was skimming—some best-selling and clever book about the one hundred greatest movies ever made—and stared at Paul. She was puzzled at first, but then she remembered him.

"Hey," she said. "It's Nonetheless."

Paul was quite sure this was the first time in the history of English that the word *nonetheless* had caused a massive erection. He fought mightily against the desire to kiss the stranger hard on the mouth.

"Wow," she said. "This is surprising, huh?"

"I can't believe you remember me," Paul said.

"I can't believe it either," she said. Then she quickly set down the book she'd been browsing. "These airport books, you know? They're entertaining crap."

Her embarrassment was lovely.

"I don't underestimate the power of popular entertainment," Paul said.

"Oh, okay, I guess," she said. "Wait, no. Let me amend that. I actually have no idea what you're talking about."

"I guess I don't either," Paul said. "I was trying to impress you with some faux philosophy."

She smiled. Paul wanted to lick her teeth. Once again, she was wearing blue jeans and a white T-shirt. Why is it that some women can turn that simple outfit into royal garb? God, he wanted her. *Want, want, want.* Can you buy and sell *want* on eBay?

"Are you still married?" he asked.

She laughed.

"Damn," she said. "You're as obvious as a thirteen-year-old. When are you going to start pawing at my breasts?"

"It's okay that you're married," he said. "I'm married, too."

"Oh, well, now, you didn't mention that the last time we met."

She was teasing him again. Mocking. Insulting. But she was not walking away. She had remembered him, had remembered a brief encounter from months earlier, and she was interested in him, in his possibilities. Wasn't she?

"No, I didn't mention my marriage," he said. "But I didn't mention it because I'm not sure how to define it. Technically speaking, I'm separated."

"Are you separated because you like to hit on strangers in airports?" she asked.

Wow. How exactly was he supposed to respond to that? He supposed his answer was going to forever change his life. Or at least decide if this woman was going to have sex with him. But he was not afraid of rejection, so why not tell the truth?

"Strictly speaking," he said, "I am not separated because I hit on strangers in airports. In fact, I can't recall another time when I hit on anybody in an airport. I am separated because I cheated on my wife."

Paul couldn't read her expression. Was she impressed or disgusted by his honesty?

"Do you have kids?" she asked.

"Three daughters. Eighteen, sixteen, and fifteen. I am surrounded by women."

"So you cheated on your daughters, not just your wife?"

Yes, it was true. Paul hated to think of it that way. But he knew his betrayal of his wife was, in some primal way, the lesser crime. What kind of message was he sending to the world when he betrayed the young women—his offspring—who would carry his name—his DNA—into the future?

"Yes," Paul said. "I cheated on my daughters. And that's pathetic. It's like I've put a letter in a bottle, and I've dropped it in the ocean, and it will someday wash up onshore, and somebody will find it, open it, and read it, and it will say, *Hello, People of the Future, my name is Paul Nonetheless, and I was a small and lonely man.*"

"You have a wife and three daughters and you still feel lonely?"

"Yes," he said. "It's true. Sad and true."

"Do you think you're as lonely, let's say, as a Russian orphan sleeping with thirty other orphans in a communal crib in the basement of a hospital in Tragikistan or somewhere?"

"No," Paul said. "I am not that lonely."

"Last week, outside of Spokane, a man and his kids got into a car wreck. He was critically injured, paralyzed from the neck down, and all five of his kids were killed. They were driving to pick up the mother at the train station. So tell me, do you think you are as lonely as that woman is right now?"

Wow, this woman had a gift for shaming!

"No," Paul said. "I am not that lonely. Not even close."

"Okay, good. You do realize that, grading on a curve, your loneliness is completely average."

"Yes, I realize that. Compared to all the lonely in the world, mine is pretty boring."

"Good," she said. "You might be an adulterous bastard, but at least you're a self-aware adulterous bastard."

She waited for his response, but he had nothing to say. He couldn't dispute the accuracy of her judgment of his questionable morals, nor could he offer her compelling evidence of his goodness. He was as she thought he was.

"My father cheated on us, too," she said. "We all knew it. My mother knew it. But he never admitted to it. He kept cheating and my mother kept ignoring it. They were married for fifty-two years and he cheated during all of them. Had to go on the damn Viagra so he could cheat well into his golden years. I think Viagra was invented so that extramarital assholes could have extra years to be assholes.

"But you know the worst thing?" she asked. "At the end, my father got cancer and he was dying and you'd think that would be the time to confess all, to get right with God, you know? But nope, on his deathbed, my father pledged his eternal and undying love to my mother. And you know what?"

"What?"

"She believed him."

Paul wanted to ask her why she doubted her father's love. Well, of course, Paul knew why she doubted it, but why couldn't her father have been telling the truth? Despite all the adultery and lies, all the shame and anger, perhaps her father had deeply and honestly loved her mother. If his last act on earth was a declaration of love, didn't that make him a loving man? Could an adulterous man also be a good man? But Paul couldn't say any of this, couldn't ask these questions. He knew it would only sound like the moral relativism of a liar, a cheater, and a thief.

"Listen to me," she said. "I can't believe I'm saying this stuff to you. I don't say this stuff to anybody, and here I am, talking to you like we're friends."

Paul figured silence was the best possible response to her candor.

"Okay, then," she said, "I guess that's it. I don't want to miss my flight. It was really nice to see you again. I'm not sure why. But it was."

She walked away. He watched her. He knew he should let her go. What attraction could he have for her now? He was the cheating husband of a cheated wife and the lying father of deceived daughters. But he couldn't let her go. Not yet. So he chased after her again.

"Hey," he said, and touched her shoulder.

"Just let me go," she said. A flash of anger. Her first flash of anger at him.

"Listen," he said. "I was going to let you go. But I couldn't. I mean, don't you think it's amazing that we've run into each other twice in two different airports?"

"It's just a coincidence."

"It's more than that. You know it's more than that. We've got some connection. I can feel it. And I think you can feel it, too."

"I have a nice ass. And a great smile. And you have pretty eyes and good hair. And you wear movie stars' clothes. That's why we noticed each other. But I have news for us, buddy, there's about two hundred women in this airport who are better-looking than me, and about two hundred and one men who are better-looking than you."

"But we've seen each other twice. And you remembered me."

"We saw each other twice because we are traveling salespeople in a capitalistic country. If we paid attention, I bet you we would notice the same twelve people over and over again."

Okay, so she was belittling him and their magical connection. And insulting his beloved country, too. But she was still talking to him. She'd tried to walk away, but he'd caught her, and she was engaged in a somewhat real conversation with him. He suddenly realized that he knew nothing of substance about this woman. He only knew her opinions of his character.

"Okay," he said. "We're making progress. I sell clothes. But you already knew that. What do you sell?"

"You don't want to know," she said.

"Yes, I do."

"No, you don't."

"Tell me."

"It will kill your dreams," she said.

That hyperbole made Paul laugh.

"Come on, it can't be that bad."

"I work for a bank," she said.

"So, wow, you're a banker," Paul said, and tried to hide his disappointment. She could have said that she did live-animal testing—smeared mascara directly into the eyes of chimpanzees—and Paul would have felt better about her career choice.

"But I'm not the kind of banker you're thinking about," she said.

"What kind of banker are you?" Paul asked, and studied her casual, if stylish, clothing. What kind of banker wore blue jeans? Perhaps a trustworthy banker? Perhaps the morality of any banker was inversely proportional to the quality of his or her clothing?

"Have you ever heard of microlending?" she asked.

"Yeah, that's where you get regular people to loan money to poor people in other countries. To start small businesses and stuff, right?"

"Basically, yes, but my company focuses on microlending to unique entrepreneurs in the United States."

"Ah, so what's your bank called?"

"We're in the start-up phase, so I don't want to get into that quite yet."

He was a little insulted, but then he realized that he was a stranger, after all, so her secrecy was understandable.

"You're just starting out then?" Paul asked. "That's why you're traveling so much?"

"Yes. We have initial funding from one source," she said, "and I'm meeting with other potential funders around the country."

"Sounds exciting," Paul said. He lied. Paul didn't trust the concept of using money to make more money. He believed it was all imaginary. He preferred his job—the selling of tangible goods. Paul trusted his merchandise. He knew a pair of blue jeans would never betray him.

"It's good work, but it's not exciting," she said. "Fund-raising is fucking humiliating. You know what I really do? You know what I'm good at? I'm good at making millionaires cry. And crying millionaires are generous with their money."

"I'm a millionaire," Paul said, "and you haven't made me cry yet."

"I haven't tried to," she said. She patted Paul on the cheek— let the hounds of condescension loose!—and walked out of the bookstore.

After she left, Paul bought the book she'd been browsing—the list of the greatest movies of all time—and read it on the flight back to Seattle. It was a book composed entirely of information taken from other sources. But Paul set it on his nightstand, then set his alarm clock on the book, and thought about the beautiful microbanker whenever he glanced at the time.

On a Tuesday, a year and a half into their separation, while sitting in their marriage counselor's office, Paul turned to his wife and tried to tell the truth.

"I love you," he said. "You're my best friend. I can't imagine a life without you as my wife. But, the thing is, I've lost my desire—my sexual desire—for you."

Could there be a more painful thing to say to her? To say to anyone? *You are not desirable.* That was a treasonous, even murderous, statement inside of a marriage. What kind of person could say that to his wife? To the person who'd most often allowed herself to be naked and vulnerable in front of him? Paul supposed he was being honest, but fuck honesty completely, fuck honesty all the way to the spine, and fuck the honest man who tells the truth on his way out the door.

"How can you say this shit to me?" she asked. "We've been separated for almost two years. You keep telling me you don't want a divorce. You keep begging me for another chance. For months, you have begged me. So here we are, Paul, this is your chance. And all you can say is that you don't desire me? What are you talking about?"

"I remember when we used to have sex all day and night," he said. "I remember we used to count your orgasms."

It was true. On a cool Saturday in early April, in the first year of their marriage, Paul had orgasmed six times while his wife had come eleven times. What had happened to those Olympian days?

"Is that the only way you can think about a marriage?" she asked. "Jesus, Paul, we were young. Our marriage was young. Everything is easier when you're young."

Paul didn't think that was true. His life had steadily improved over the years and, even in the middle of a marital blowup, Paul was still pleased with his progress and place in the world.

"I don't know why I feel the way I do," Paul said. "I just feel that way. I feel like we have gone cold to each other."

"I haven't gone cold," she said. "I'm burning, okay? You know how long it's been since I've had sex? It's been almost four years. Four years! And you know what? I'm ashamed to say that aloud. Listen to me. I'm ashamed that I'm still married to the man who has not fucked me in four years."

Paul looked to the marriage counselor for help. He felt lost in the ocean of his wife's rage and needed a friggin' lifeguard. But the counselor sat in silence. In *learned* silence, the bastard.

"Don't you have anything to say?" she asked Paul. "I'm your wife. I'm the mother of your children. I deserve some respect. No, I demand it. I demand your respect."

He wanted to tell her the truth. He wanted to tell himself the truth, really. But was he capable of such a thing? Could he tell her what he suspected? Could he share his theory about the loss of desire? If he sang to her, would that make it easier? Is honesty easier in four/four time?

"Are you just going to sit there?" she asked. "Is this what it comes down to, you sitting there?"

My love, he wanted to say to her, I began to lose my desire for you during the birth of our first child, and it was gone by the birth of our third. Something happened to me in those delivery rooms. I saw too much. I saw your body do things—I saw it change—and I have not been able to look at you, to see you naked, without remembering all the blood and pain and fear. *All the changes.* I was terrified. I thought you were dying. I felt like I was in the triage room of a wartime hospital, and there was nothing I could do. I felt so powerless. I felt like I was failing you. I know it's irrational. Jesus, I know it's immature and ignorant and completely irrational. *I know it's wrong.* I should have told you that I didn't want to be in the delivery room for the first birth. And I should have never been in the delivery room during the second and third. Maybe my desire would have survived, would have recovered, if I had not seen the second and third births. Maybe I wouldn't feel like such a failure. But how was I supposed to admit to these things? In the twenty-first-century United States, what kind of father and husband chooses not to be in the delivery room?

My love, Paul wanted to say, I am a small and lonely man made smaller and lonelier by my unspoken fears.

"Paul!" his wife screamed. "Talk to me!"

"I don't know," Paul said. "I don't know why I feel this way. I just do."

"Paul." The counselor finally spoke, finally had an opinion. "Have you considered that your lack of desire might be a physical issue? Have you consulted a doctor about this? There are—"

"He has no problem fucking other women," she said. "He's fucked plenty of other women. He just has a problem fucking me."

She was right. Even now, as they fought to save their marriage, Paul was thinking of the woman in the airport. He was thinking about all other women and not the woman in his life.

That night, on eBay, Paul bid on a suit once worn by Sean Connery during the publicity tour for *Thunderball*. It would be too big for Paul; Connery is a big man. But Paul still wanted it. Maybe he'd frame it and put it on the wall of his apartment. Maybe he'd drink martinis and stare at it. Maybe he'd imagine that a crisp white pocket square made all the difference in the world. But he lost track of the auction and lost the suit to somebody whose screen name was Shaken, Not Stirred.

Jesus, Paul thought, I'm wasting my life.

After the divorce, Paul's daughters spent every other weekend with him. It was not enough time. It would never be enough. And he rarely saw them during his weekends anyway because they were teenagers. Everywhere he looked, he saw happy men—good and present fathers—and he was not one of them. A wealthy man, an educated man, a privileged man, he had failed his family—his children—as easily and brutally as the poorest, most illiterate, and helpless man in the country. And didn't that prove the greatness of the United States? All of us wealthy and imperial Americans are the children of bad fathers! Ha! thought Paul. Each of us—rich and poor, gay and straight, black and white—we are fragile and finite. We all go through this glorious life without guarantees, without promise of rescue or redemption. We have freedom of speech and religion, and the absolute freedom to leave behind our loved ones, to force them to unhappily pursue us. How can I possibly protect my daughters from their nightmares, from their waking fears, Paul thought, if I am not sleeping in the room next door? Oh, God, he missed them! Pure and simple, he ached. But who has sympathy for the failed father? Who sings honor songs for the monster?

And what could he do for his daughters? He could outfit them in gorgeous vintage clothing. So he gave them dresses and shoes and pants that were worn by Doris Day, Marilyn Monroe, and Audrey Hepburn.

"Who is Audrey Hepburn?" his youngest daughter had asked.

"She was perfect," Paul said.

"But who is she?"

"An actress. A movie star."

"What movies has she been in?"

"I don't think you've seen any of them."

"If I don't know who she is, why did you buy me her dress?"

It was a good question. Paul didn't have an answer. He just looked at this young woman in front of him—his daughter—and felt powerless.

"I thought maybe if you wore different clothes at school," Paul said, "maybe you could start a trend. You'd be original."

"Oh, my God," she said. "It's high school, Dad. People get beat up for being original."

Jesus, Paul had thought he was giving her social capital. He thought he could be a microlender of art—the art of the pop song. So he gave music to his daughters. Yes, he'd once romanced their mother with mix tapes, dozens of mix tapes, so he'd romance his daughters—in an entirely different way—with iPods. So Paul bought three iPods and loaded them with a thousand songs each. Three iPods, three thousand songs. Instead of just a few songs on a CD or a cassette tape, Paul had made epic mixes. Paul had given each daughter a third of his musical history. And, oh, they were delighted—were ecstatic—when they opened their gifts and saw new iPods, but, oh, how disappointed—how disgusted—they were when they discovered that their new iPods were already filled with songs, songs chosen by their father. By their sad and desperate father.

"Daddy," his eldest daughter said. "Why did you put all *your* music on here?"

"I chose all those songs for you," he said. "They're specifically for you."

"But all these songs are *your* songs," she said. "They're not mine."

"But if you listen to them," he said, "if you learn them, then maybe they can become *our* songs."

"We don't have to love the same things," she said.

"But I want you to love what I love."

Did I say that? Paul asked himself. Did I just sound that love starved and socially inept? Am I intimidated by my own daughter? In place of romantic love for my wife, am I trying to feel romantic love for my daughters? No, no, no, no, Paul thought. But he wasn't sure. How could he be sure? He was surrounded by women he did not understand.

"It's okay, Daddy," she said. "I can just load my music over your music. Thank you for the iPod."

She shook her head—a dismissive gesture she'd learned from her mother—kissed her incompetent father on the cheek, and left the room.

Three years after his divorce had finalized, after two of his daughters had gone off to college, one to Brown and the other to Oberlin, and his third daughter had disowned him, Paul saw Sara Smile again in the Detroit Airport. They saw each other at the same time, both walking toward a coffee kiosk.

"Sara Smile," he said.

"Excuse me?" the woman said.

"It's me," he said. "Paul Nonetheless."

"I'm sorry," she said. "Do I know you?"

He realized this woman only looked like his Sara Smile. It would have been too much to ask for a third chance meeting. If he'd run into Sara Smile again, they would have had to make their way over to the airport hotel—the Hyatt or Hilton or whatever it was—and get a room. He could imagine them barely making it inside the door before their hands were down each other's pants. God, he'd drop to his knees, unbutton her pants, pull them down to her ankles, and kiss her thighs. He'd pull aside her panties and push his mouth against her crotch and she'd want it for a few moments—she'd moan her approvals—and then she'd remember her husband and her life—substantial—and she'd push Paul away. She'd pull up her pants and apologize and rush out of the room. And Paul would be there, alone again, on his knees again, in a room where thousands of people had slept, eaten, fucked, and made lonely phone calls home. And who would Paul call? Who was waiting for his voice on the line? But wait, none of this had happened. It wasn't real. Paul was still standing in the Detroit Airport next to a woman—a stranger—who only strongly resembled Sara Smile.

"Are you going to call this coincidental now?" he asked this stranger.

"You have me confused with somebody else," she said. She was smiling. She was enjoying this odd and humorous interaction with the eccentric man in his old-fashioned suit.

"Can I buy you a coffee?" he asked. He knew she was the wrong woman. But he wasn't going to let that become an impediment.

"Sir," she said. "I'm not who you think I am."

She wasn't smiling now. She realized that something was wrong with this man. Yes, she was in an airport, surrounded by people—by security—but she was still a little afraid.

"How's your marriage?" he asked.

"Sir, please," she said. "Stop bothering me."

She walked away, but Paul followed her. He couldn't stop himself. He needed her. He walked a few feet behind her.

"Me asking about your marriage is just a way of talking about my marriage," he said. "But you knew that, right? Anyway, I'm divorced now."

"Sir, if you don't leave me alone, I am going to find a cop."

She stopped and put her hands up as if to ward off a punch.

"My wife left me," Paul said. "Or I left her. We left each other. It's hard to say who left first."

Paul shrugged his shoulders. And then he sang the first few bars of "She's Gone." But he couldn't quite hit Daryl Hall's falsetto notes.

"I can't hit those high notes," Paul said. "But it's not about the notes, is it? It's about the heat behind the notes."

"What's wrong with you?" the woman asked.

Two hours later, Paul sat in a simple room at a simple table while two men in suits leaned against the far wall and studied him.

"I'm not a terrorist," Paul said. "If that's what you're thinking."

The men didn't speak. Maybe they couldn't speak. Maybe there were rules against speaking. Maybe this was some advanced interrogation technique. Maybe they were silent because they knew Paul would want to fill the room with his voice.

"Come on, guys," he said. "I got a little carried away. I knew it wasn't her. I knew it wasn't Sara. I just needed to pretend for a while. Just a few moments. If she'd let me buy her some coffee or something. If she'd talked to me, everything would have been okay."

The men whispered to each other.

Paul decided it might be best if he stopped talking, if he stopped trying to explain himself.

Instead he would sing. Yes, he would find the perfect song for this situation and he would sing it. And these men—police officers, federal agents, mysterious suits—would recognize the song. They certainly wouldn't (or couldn't) sing along, but they'd smile and nod their heads in recognition. They'd share a moment with Paul. They'd have a common history, maybe even a common destiny. Rock music had that kind of power. But what song? What song would do?

And Paul knew—understood with a bracing clarity—that he must sing Marvin Gaye's "What's Going On." And so he began to hum at first, finding the tune, before he sang the first few lyrics—mumbled them, really, because he couldn't quite remember them—but when he came to the chorus, Paul belted it out. He sang loudly, and his imperfect, ragged vocals echoed in that small and simple room.

What's going on?
What's going on?
What's going on?

And, yes, Paul recognized that his singing—his spontaneous talent show—could easily be seen as troublesome. It could even be seen as crazy. Paul knew he wasn't crazy. He was just sad, very sad. And he was trying to sing his way out of the sadness.

What's going on?
What's going on?
What's going on?

The men kept staring at Paul. They wouldn't smile. They wouldn't even acknowledge the song. Why not? But then Paul remembered what had happened to Marvin Gaye. Broken, depressed, alcoholic, drug-addicted, Marvin had ended up living back home with his parents. Even as his last hit, "Sexual Healing," was selling millions of copies, Marvin was sleeping in his parents' house.

And, oh, how Marvin fought with his father. Day after day, Marvin Gaye Sr. and Marvin Gaye Jr. *screamed* at each other.

"What happened to you?"

"It's all your fault."

"You had it all and you lost it."

"You're wasting your life."

"Where's my money?"

"You have stolen from me."

"You owe me."

"I don't owe you shit."

Had any father and son ever disappointed each other so completely? But Paul couldn't stop singing. Even as he remembered that Marvin Gaye Sr. had shot and killed his son—killed his song.

What's going on?

What's going on?

What's going on?

And then it was over. Paul stopped singing. This was the wrong song. Yes, it was the worst possible song to be singing at this moment. There had to be a better one, but Paul couldn't think of it, couldn't even think of another inappropriate song. *What's wrong with me? Why can't I remember?* Paul laughed at himself as he sat in the airport interrogation room. How had he come to this? Wasn't Paul a great man who lived in a great country? Hadn't he succeeded? Jesus, he was good at everything he had ever attempted. Well, he had failed at marriage, but couldn't he be good at grief? Couldn't he be an all-star griever? Couldn't he, through his own fierce tears, tell his captors that he wasn't going to die? Couldn't he survive? Couldn't he pause now and rest his voice—rest his soul—and then start singing again when he felt strong enough? Could he do that? Was he ever going to be that strong?

"Officers," Paul said, "I'm very tired. Can I please have some time? The thing is, I'm sorry for everything. And I know this is no excuse, but I think—I realize now that I want to remember everything—every song, every article of clothing—because I'm afraid they will be forgotten."

One of the men shook his head; the other turned his back and spoke into a cell phone.

Paul bowed his head with shame.

And then he spoke so softly that he wasn't sure the men heard him. Paul thought of his wife and his daughters, of Sara Smile, and he said, "I don't want to be forgotten. I don't want to be forgotten. Don't forget me. Don't forget me. Don't forget me. Don't forget me."

On Airplanes

I am always amused
By those couples—

Lovers and spouses—
Who perform and ask

Others to perform
Musical chairs

Whenever they, by
Random seat selection,

Are separated
From each other.

"Can you switch
Seats with me?"

A woman asked me.
"So I can sit

With my husband?"
She wanted me,

A big man, who
Always books early,

And will gratefully
Pay extra for the exit row,

To trade my aisle seat
For her middle seat.

By asking me to change
My location for hers,

The woman is actually
Saying to me:

"Dear stranger, dear
Sir, my comfort is

More important than yours.
Dear solitary traveler,

My love and fear—
As contained

Within my marriage—
Are larger than yours."

O, the insult!
O, the condescension!

And this is not
An isolated incident.

I've been asked
To trade seats

Twenty or thirty times
Over the years.

How dare you!
How dare you

Ask me to change
My life for you!

How imperial!
How colonial!

But, ah, here is
The strange truth:

Whenever I'm asked
To trade seats

For somebody else's love,
I do, I always do.

BIG BANG THEORY

After our earliest ancestors crawled out of the oceans, how soon did they feel the desire to crawl back in?

At age nine, I stepped into the pool at the YWCA. I didn't know how to swim, but the other Indian boys had grown salmon and eagle wings and could fly in water and sky.

Wouldn't the crow, that ubiquitous trickster, make a more compelling and accurate national symbol for the United States than the bald eagle?

Okay, that Indian-boy salmon-and-eagle-wings transformation thing is bullshit, but I'm trying to tell a creation story here, and by definition all creation stories are bullshit. Scientifically speaking, we all descend from one man and woman who lived in what we now call Africa—yes, we are all African at our cores—but why should we all live with the same metaphorical creation story? The Kiowa think they were created when lightning struck the mud inside a log. I think the Hopis are crash-landed aliens who are still waiting for a rescue mission. Christians think God built everything in a week—well, in six days—and then rested. Yeah, like God created the universe in anticipation of the Sunday funny pages.

*Q: In the singles bar, over nonalcoholic beer, what did the Palestin-
ian say to the Israeli?*
A: "Your holy war or mine?"

But wait, before I get too critical or metaphysical, let me return
to that YWCA on Maple Street in Spokane, Washington. I stood
alone in the shallow end while my big brother, cousins, best
friend, and little warrior enemies swam in the deep end. I was so
ashamed, but then our female swim instructors shouted my name
and challenged me to dive off the five-foot board. Fuck that! I
jumped out of the pool and ran into the locker room.

*There is a myth that drowning is a peaceful death. I've heard people
say, "I would just open my mouth and breathe death in." In truth,
drowning is torture. The fear of drowning is used as torture.*

At the YWCA, I quickly dressed and waited for the other Indian boys, who mocked me for my aquatic cowardice and
locked me in a towel bin. But I escaped and made it onto the bus
that took us to the Fox Theater for a matinee showing of *Jaws*,
the blockbuster that changed the way our country looks at
sharks and at films.

Did you know that when a shark stops swimming, it dies?

As we walked past the endless line of movie lovers, the other
boys kept pitching me crap, but then our female swim instructors, one Japanese and one Korean, shouted my name again and
insisted that I join them in the line. "But what about us?" my
brother asked. "You go to the deep end," the Japanese girl said.

Big Bang Theory

A wise man once said that revenge is not more important than love or compassion. Until it is.

I was nine. The Asian girls were sixteen. I sat between them and they each held one of my hands as we watched a great white shark devour people. At one point, when a little boy was in danger, I hid my face in the Korean girl's chest. Oh, it was the first time I had ever been that close to a woman's breast.

Do you think the universe is expanding or contracting?

I wish I knew what happened to those Asian girls. Are they still living in Spokane? Do you realize how much they mean to me? Did they love me? Or was I just a sad-ass kid who needed their help? If I could talk to them, I would tell them this creation story: "A bonnethead shark in Omaha, Nebraska, conceived and gave birth to a baby that soon died. But this mother shark had never shared water with a male. Scientists were puzzled. So they performed a DNA test and discovered the dead baby only had its mother's DNA. Yes, that bonnethead shark had given virgin birth. Do you think this is amazing? Well, it's not. Dozens of species of insects give virgin birth. Crayfish give virgin birth. Some honeybees give virgin birth. And Komodo dragons—yeah, those big lizards give virgin birth, too. Jeez, one human gives virgin birth and that jump-starts one of the world's great religions. But when a Komodo dragon gives virgin birth, do you know what it's thinking? It's thinking, *This is Tuesday, right? I think this is Tuesday. What am I going to do on Wednesday?*

Ode for Pay Phones

All

That

Autumn,

I walked from

The apartment (shared

With my sisters) to that pay phone

On Third Avenue, next to a sleazy gas station

And down the block from the International House of Pan-
cakes. I was working the night

Shift at a pizza joint and you were away at college. You dated a
series of inconsequential boys. Well, each boy meant little on his

Own, but their cumulative effect devastated my brain and
balls. I wanted you to stop kissing relative strangers, so I called
you at midnight as often as I could afford. If I talked to you
that late, I knew

(Or hoped) you couldn't rush into anybody's bed. But, O, I still recall the misery of hearing the *ring, ring, ring, ring*

Of your unanswered phone. These days, I'd text you to find you, but where's the delicious pain

In that? God, I miss standing in the mosquito dark

At this or that pay phone. I wish

That I could find one

And call back

All that

I

Loved.

FEARFUL SYMMETRY

When he was eighteen and a senior in high school, Sherwin Polatkin and a group of his schoolmates jumped into two cars and drove into Spokane to see *The Breakfast Club*. Sherwin sat next to Karen, a smart and confident sophomore—a farm-town white girl with the sun-bleached hair and tanned skin of a harvest truck driver. She'd never been of romantic interest, so Sherwin slouched in his seat and munched on popcorn. It was just the random draw of a dozen friends choosing seats.

But near the end of the movie, as Molly Ringwald and Judd Nelson were making out in a supply closet, Sherwin was surprised to discover that Karen was holding his hand and even more surprised when she started playing with his fingers. Their friends had no idea this was happening. Karen lightly ran her fingertips along Sherwin's palm, the backs of his fingers, and his wrist. It was simple—and nearly innocent—but it still felt like sex.

Sherwin was not a virgin—he'd had sex with three girls—but this was the first time a girl had been so indirect with her desires. He'd touched naked women, but this hand-holding—this skin against skin—seemed far more intimate. He loved it. He was a Spokane Indian, the lead singer for his drum group, and had a sudden urge to sing an honor song for Karen—for her tenderness. He was nervous they'd be discovered. He knew their friends would be both titillated and slightly offended by this contact. It seemed like a betrayal of what was otherwise a platonic gathering. But Sherwin could not stop it. And Karen certainly didn't want to stop it. He would never touch her again, and they would never speak of the moment and would not see each other again after high school, but Sherwin always considered it one of the best moments of his life.

So, years later, when he became a professional writer, Sherwin would tell curious journalists that he loved movies and his favorite movie of all time was *The Breakfast Club,* but he would never tell them why. He knew that the best defense against fame was keeping certain secrets. He hoped that Karen, wherever she was, would someday read an interview with him and smile when she read about his cinematic preference.

On August 11, 1948, sixteen smoke jumpers, led by a taciturn man named Wayne Ford, parachuted into Sirois Canyon, a remote area near Wenatchee, Washington, to fight a small wildfire. However, the fire, unpredictable as such fires can be, exploded into a fifty-foot-tall wall of flame, jumped the canyon, and chased the smoke jumpers up a steep and grassy hillside. Fifteen smoke jumpers tried to outrun the fire, an impossible race to win, but Wayne Ford didn't run. Instead, he did something that was new and crazy: He built the first U.S. Forest Service escape fire.

Did you know that you can escape a fire by setting another fire at your feet? You might seem to be building a funeral pyre, but you're creating a circle of safety. In order to save your endangered ass, all you have to do is burn down the grass surrounding you, lie facedown in the ash, and pray that the bigger fire will pass over you like a flock of blind and burning angels.

I know you're thinking, *You're crazy. There's no way I'm going to set a fire when another fire is already chasing me.* And that's exactly what Wayne Ford's men thought. They had never seen any firefighter set one fire to escape another. It was unprecedented—for white folks. Indians had set many such escape fires before white men had arrived in the Americas, but Wayne Ford and his men had no way of knowing this.

Wise Wayne Ford—who before the fire had the same color and sinewy bite as one hundred and fifty pounds of deer jerky—could never fully explain why he set his escape fire. All he ever said is that it just made sense. Ford's men tried to outrun the murderous flames, but one by one they all succumbed to the fire and smoke. Ford calmly lay down in the ash, in his circle of safety, and lived.

Thirty years after the Sirois Canyon fire, Harris Tolkin, a former smoke jumper, began to write a nonfiction chronicle of the tragedy, *Fearful Symmetry: The True Story of the Sirois Canyon Fire.* Tolkin borrowed the title of his book from the first and last stanzas of William Blake's most famous poem:

> Tyger! Tyger! burning bright
> In the forests of the night,
> What immortal hand or eye
> Could frame thy fearful symmetry?

In exploring the meanings of the Sirois Canyon fire and its aftermath, Tolkin relied heavily on William Blake's notions of *innocence* and *experience* and on the dichotomies of joy and sorrow, childhood and adulthood, religious faith and doubt, and good and evil. Tolkin died before completing the book, but it was edited by his daughter, Diane Tolkin, and was posthumously published in 2002 and was a surprise *New York Times* best seller for twenty-six weeks. In 2003, Tesla Studios, fresh off a Best Picture Oscar for their Civil War epic, *Leaves of Grass,* approached a hot young short-story writer, poet and first-time screenwriter, Sherwin Polatkin, to adapt *Fearful Symmetry* for the big screen.

Sitting in the Tesla offices, Sherwin stared through a glass desk at the bare feet of the executive producer, a short thin man who was otherwise completely dressed in a gorgeous bespoke suit.

"So, Sherwin," the producer said, "why are you here?"

That was a strange question, considering that Sherwin had been invited. He decided that it must be an existential query. Or no, maybe it was just the first question of a job interview. This was Hollywood, yes, but Sherwin was really just a typist—a *creative* typist—trying to get a job.

"Well, number one," Sherwin said, "I know fire like no other screenwriter in this town. I was a hotshot, a forest firefighter, for ten summers. It's how I paid for college."

That was a lie. Sherwin had only fought one fire in his life— a burning hay bale—and he'd only had to pour ten buckets of water on it. But this executive had no way of knowing Sherwin was a liar. Wasn't everybody in Hollywood a liar? Maybe Sherwin could only distinguish himself by the quality of his lies and not their quantity.

"And number two, I'm a Native American," Sherwin said. "I'm indigenous to the West, to the idea of the West, and you're not going to find that sort of experience in film school."

That couldn't be true. Wasn't Hollywood filled with small-town folks from the West—hell, from everywhere? Wasn't Hollywood filled with nomads? Yes, Jewish folks, those original nomads, created the movie business, and it had not really changed in all the decades since, had it? Wasn't Sherwin really just one more nomad in a business filled with nomads? How could he really distinguish himself?

"Listen," Sherwin said to the executive, "I'm nervous and I'm exaggerating, and I'm sounding like an arrogant bastard, so let's just start over. Is that okay? Can we call *cut* and start this scene over? Can we do a reshoot?"

The executive smiled and tugged at his toes. Yes, they were well-manicured toes, but it was still disconcerting, in the context of a business meeting, to see something—ten things—so naked and—well, toelike.

"We've had about a dozen screenwriters work on this project," the executive said. "And had three different directors attached. And none of them could crack this thing. So tell me, how are you going to crack it?"

Sherwin didn't quite understand the terminology. He assumed it had something to do with secret codes and languages. So he went with that.

"Well, the book itself is a tragedy." Sherwin said.

"Tragedies are fucked at the box office," the executive said.

Sherwin didn't know if that was true. It didn't feel true. Or maybe it was truer than Sherwin wanted to believe. Weren't

Americans afraid of tragedy? As a Native American, Sherwin was, by definition, trapped in a difficult but lustful marriage with tragedy. But that cultural fact wouldn't get him this job.

"I think there's redemption in this story," Sherwin said. "I know I can find the redemption."

"Redemption," the executive said. "Yes, that's exactly what we need."

Thus hired on the basis of one word—one universal concept—Sherwin tried to transform a tragedy into a redemptive action-adventure movie. How did he go about his task? First he pulled the story out of the past and reset it in the present. Why? Because the studio thought the audience wouldn't watch another period piece, and because the director—an old studio pro who was rumored to have had sex with at least three of the actresses who'd starred in *Dallas*, the TV series—wanted his Chinese girlfriend to play the female lead. Ah, the things one does for diversity!

But in changing the time frame of the Sirois Canyon fire at the behest of the capitalistic studio and the love-struck director, Polatkin was confronted with a logical problem. If the fictional Wayne Ford were to set an escape fire in 2003 and still be ignored by his crew members for such a crazy idea, Polatkin would have to pretend that forest-fire fighters still didn't know about escape fires. This, of course, was a nasty insult to the intelligence of firefighters. So Polatkin only had one option. He had to change the narrative and eliminate Wayne Ford's escape fire—or, rather, the concept of a man setting the first escape fire in U.S. Forest Service history. But Harris Tolkin's book revolves around the revolutionary nature of this escape fire. Thus, by eliminating the escape fire and its aftermath, Polatkin created a screenplay that had little connection to the narrative and moral concerns of the sourcebook.

Such are the dangers of creating art based on other art. Such are the dangers of Hollywood, where it is contractually understood that screenwriters will write first drafts with verve, and then, with each revision, lose more nerve and individuality. It's fucked, but Polatkin got paid five hundred thousand bucks to write a first draft where the killing fire burned as brightly as William Blake's tygers. In fact, Wayne Ford, younger and renamed for the film, saw tygers inside the flames as they chased his team up the steep slope. The others lost all innocence and hope and died before they reached the summit. But Ford reached the top and made the mad plummet down the back slope with the fire tygers in pursuit. He didn't build an escape fire—no time for that old tactic—he just ran, and he survived because he was so damn fast.

There is real inspiration for this fictional flight from fiery death. On July 3, 1999, near Boulder, Colorado, another relatively small wildfire exploded into a conflagration and chased sixteen firefighters up a steep slope and killed fifteen of them. Only Richard McPhee, an experienced smoke jumper out of Bonners Ferry, Idaho, was able to outrun the flames. Later, when researchers did the math, they estimated that McPhee ran the equivalent of a hundred-yard dash in nine seconds. That would be a world-record speed on a *flat* surface, but McPhee ran it while carrying a forty-pound backpack up a heavily forested sixty-degree slope. The man *wanted* to live. It gives one pleasure to take the measure of a man's fight to survive. Ask yourself: Could I have run that fast and won the right to live? This might be glib, but certain men are born to be stars—to be at their best when faced with death. Richard McPhee only believes he was lucky.

"Yeah, I've got speed," he said. "But hell, what if I had fallen or tripped or just hit some bad luck? What if I had started in back and had to run past everyone? I lived because nobody was running slowly in front of me."

Richard McPhee refuses to be called a hero, which makes him the perfect real-life model for a cinematic star. So, in writing his first-draft screenplay, Polatkin blended aspects of Wayne Ford and Richard McPhee's heroism and created an entirely fictional smoke jumper, now named Joseph Adams, who survived a murderous inferno but was emotionally and spiritually crippled by survivor's guilt. Angry and drinking alcoholically, Joseph Adams falls apart in the first act, staggers his way through the second act, and finds redemption in the third act when he again faces a monster fire but sacrifices his own life to save his entire team, including the love of his life, a Vietnamese-American smoke jumper named Grace. Yes, Sherwin decided that the director's Chinese girlfriend would cross over racial borders and play a Vietnamese-American woman, a first-generation immigrant, who had fled the Vietnam War and was adopted and raised by a white American family. And yes, Polatkin, the possessor of a reservation-inspired messiah complex ("I am the smartest Indian in the universe and I will save all you other Indians!"), decided that the hero, Joseph Adams, should die so that others might live.

Okay, Polatkin wasn't writing Shakespeare, but he did write an interesting screenplay, maybe even a good one. But as he'd feared, the studio had notes. They wanted to change a few things so Polatkin flew to Hollywood, met his town-car driver, and was driven to a meeting room in L.A. Sherwin kept thinking of Survivor's eighties hit, "Eye of the Tiger," as twenty studio executives shuttled into the room. The director, angry because his other project had been scuttled, rolled in late, stuffed his face with a muffin, and said, while spewing food, "This screenplay is seriously flawed, but it's nothing we can't fix."

The director was wearing cargo shorts. Sherwin was convinced that nobody over the age of thirty-three should ever wear cargo shorts.

For the rest of the day, the director and the executives made suggestions and demands: "The hero can't die. Get rid of the William Blake shit. And you need more action, more fistfights and fucking. Maybe you could write a scene where the hero fucks his girl in the ash after a fire. The hero could leave ashy handprints on his girl's back—on her whole body. That would be primal and hot. Jesus, it would be poetry."

Polatkin fought for his screenplay's survival, but it was a pathetic and lonely battle. He was a writer-for-hire and was contractually bound to follow studio orders or he would be fired and replaced. So, feeling hollow and violated, he took careful notes as a roomful of businessmen wrested art into commodity. He thought of how much he had always loved movies and how, for most his life, he'd had no idea how they were made. He thought of the boy he had been, sitting in that dark theater with Karen, the girl from high school, and how innocent it was.

Not perfect, not at all, but better—cleaner—than this meeting. How had the boy who loved movies become so different from this man who wrote them?

And then Sherwin saw the latest issue of *The New Yorker*, crisp and unread, on the table. He had just published his first short story in the magazine. It's every fiction writer's wish to be published in the same magazine that has published Cheever, Munro, Yates, and ten thousand other greats and near-greats and goods.

"Hey," Sherwin said. "I've got a short story in that *New Yorker*."

The director flipped through the magazine, coughed and sighed, and said, "You should let me be your editor because you would win the fucking Pulitzer if I were in charge of your career."

The room went cold and silent. The professionally cold studio executives couldn't believe that any human being, even a film director, had said something so deluded and imperial.

Polatkin was baffled. No, it was worse than that. At that moment, something broke inside him. He didn't know it at the time, but he'd fractured some part of his soul. He only realized the extent of his spiritual injuries a few months later. While writing nine drafts of the screenplay, Sherwin—who had already taken out the concept of the first escape fire set in U.S. Forest Service history—discovered that he could not take the William Blake out of a book whose title and themes were based on Blake's poetry.

"I can't do it," he said to the director. "The book is about Blake. How can you take Blake out if the book is about Blake?"

"Fuck Blake," the director said. "And fuck this book. Do you think this book is the fucking Bible? Do you think it's sacred? Jesus, we're making a movie, and that's more fucking important than this book. I'm going to make a movie that's ten times—a hundred times—greater than this fucking book. So are you going to take out the fucking Blake or what?"

"I can't do it," Sherwin said.

"Then fuck you. You're fired."

It was easy to fire screenwriters. But Sherwin was not just a screenwriter. He was also the author of a book of short stories and two volumes of poetry, and he still wanted to explore the notion of heroic self-sacrifice, so he decided to write a series of sonnets dedicated to smoke jumpers. At his home in San Francisco, he sat at his computer and stared at the blank screen. He sat, silent and unworking, for hours, for weeks, for months. Every time he tried to write a word, a metaphor, a line of poetry, he could only hear the critical voices of the studio executives and the director: *The hero can't die. Get rid of the William Blake shit.* Sherwin had fallen victim to his own imagination. He couldn't create anything on the page, but he was fully capable of creating fictional and aural ghosts who prevented him from writing.

Desperate, he decided the computer's advanced technology was creating the impediment. He decided to go back to the beginning—to the Adam and Eve of writing—the pen and paper. Yes, he tried to write by hand. He reasoned that if Herman Melville could write *Moby-fucking-Dick* with an inky feather, he could write one measly goddamn sonnet with a felt tip pen and

graph paper. But he could still hear the executives and director talking. *The hero can't die. Get rid of the William Blake shit.*
He was suffering from Hollywood-induced schizophrenia and
couldn't produce a word. Polatkin had always mocked those
folks who'd claimed to suffer from writer's block. But now, he
was a writer . . .

Who could not produce one goddamn word.
The poems had migrated like goddamn birds.
And no matter what you may have heard,
Writer's block causes physical hurt.
The fool couldn't wear a goddamn shirt
Because the cotton scratched, bruised, and burned
His skin. His stomach ached; his vision blurred.
What happens to a soul that's shaken *and* stirred?

What happens to a writer who can't write?
Who flees his office and drives through the night,
In search of some solace, some goddamn streetlight
That will illuminate and give back his life,
His odes and lyrics? The desperate fool tried
Every workshop trick. The agnostic fool cried
To God for relief. God, can a man die
Of writer's block? Well, the fool did survive

. . . the early and most painful stages of his creative disease.
Sherwin grew numb. He became strangely complacent with
the idea that he would never write again. Oh, Sherwin still
loved words, but he found other ways to play with them. He
discovered the magic and terror of crossword puzzles. He read

dictionaries and encyclopedias that promised to help him solve
the most difficult ones. He soon became good at crossword
puzzles. By testing himself using the same crosswords the best
puzzlers solved in competition, Sherwin learned that he was
probably one of the best five hundred crossword puzzle solvers in the English-speaking world.

He'd become that good after only six months of part-time
work. How good could he become if he dedicated himself fully
to the task? He figured that by living even more frugally than
he had for the last decade, he had enough cash to survive for
one more decade. So he decided to become, for lack of a better
term, a crossword monk. But instead of praying, instead of
keeping a diary, instead of transcribing by hand every page of
some holy book, Sherwin made lists of words, the most common crossword-puzzle answers:

AREA	OLE
ERA	IRE
ERE	ESE
ELI	ENE
ALE	ARE
ALOE	ATE
EDEN	NEE
ALI	ALA
ETA	AGE
ESS	IRA
ERIE	ACE
ANTE	ELSE
ARIA	ODE

ERR	EVE
ADO	ETNA
IDEA	ASEA
EEL	ASH
END	ANTI
ANT	EAR
APE	ARI
ACRE	ETAL
EST	

That was just the short list. There were a thousand or more common answers. They were the building blocks of crossword puzzles. But the quality—the comedy and tragedy—of a puzzle often had less to do with the answers than with the clues. A great solver understood the poetry of the clues. The most difficult puzzles used puns, misdirection, verb-noun elision, and camouflage in their clueing.

Sherwin believed himself to be a great solver, so he traveled to the American Crossword Puzzle Championship in Stamford, Connecticut.

When he stepped into the conference room, crowded with solvers who all seemed to know one another, Sherwin was nervous and vaguely ashamed of himself. Was this what his life had come to? He'd been flying first class to Hollywood, and now he was paying too much for a king bed nonsmoking in a Hilton in Connecticut? Yes, it was a wealthy, lovely, and privileged part of the state, but it still felt like a descent.

But wait, Sherwin thought, stop judging people. These solvers were a group of people who had to be clever. These people were thinkers. Yes, there had to be plenty of eccentrics—compulsive hand-washers, functioning autistics, encyclopedia readers, and compulsive cat collectors—but didn't that actually make them a highly attractive group of people? When had Sherwin been anything other than a weird fucker? Didn't he get paid to be a weird fucker?

"Hello," he said to the woman at the registration desk. She wore a name tag with her name, *Sue*, spelled out on a crossword grid.

"Hello," Sue said. "Welcome to the tournament. Are you a contestant or a journalist?"

"A contestant."

"So this must be your first time here?" she asked.

"How do you know that?"

"Oh, this is a family, really, a highly dysfunctional family." She laughed. "I know everybody. But I don't know you. So that makes you new."

"You've got me."

"Okay, I'll sign you up for the C Group."

"C? What's that?"

"It's for new solvers."

"I'm new," Sherwin said, "but I'm good."

"Oh, first-timers are always C Group. If you do well enough on the first few puzzles, they'll consider moving you up right away, but that rarely happens."

"Why not?"

"Because the puzzles are always more difficult than you'd expect. And because the pressure—well, first-timers have no idea how much pressure there is. And—well, they tend to choke a bit."

Sue laughed again.

"Are you laughing at me?" Sherwin asked.

"Oh, no," she said. "I'm sorry. I'm laughing at myself. I've been coming to this tournament for seventeen years and I'm still a C Group. I keep choking year after year."

"I'm used to pressure."

"Oh, I'm not judging you. It's all supposed to be fun. It *is* fun. Just sign up with the C Group and have fun. This is your first time. You have years of fun ahead of you."

Years of fun? When had anybody ever said such a thing and meant it? Sue meant it. Sherwin shrugged and signed up for C Group.

Later that afternoon, he sat at a long table in a room filled with long tables. He had four pencils and a good eraser. He sat beside an elderly Korean woman who looked as if she'd been born in her sweater.

"Hello," she said. "You must be new?"

She had a slight accent, so she was probably a first-generation immigrant. She'd probably been in the United States for twenty-five years. She'd been here long enough to become a crossword solver. Sherwin realized that he had no idea if crossword puzzles were written in other languages. Were other languages flexible enough?

"Are you new?" the Korean woman asked again. She was missing a lower front tooth. This made her look somehow younger, even impish. Don't be condescending, Sherwin chastised himself.

"Yes, I'm new," he said. "C Group."

"Welcome, welcome," she said. "We're like a family here."

"So I've heard."

"Yes, just like a family. Like my family. My big sister is a legendary bitch. Just like that bitch over there."

She pointed a pencil at another elderly woman, a white woman wearing thick glasses. Didn't she know that one could purchase plastic lenses these days?

"Why is she a bitch?" Sherwin asked.

"Because she always beats me. And because she always apologizes for beating me. Young man, you must never apologize for being good. It makes the rest of us feel worse about ourselves."

"Okay, good advice," Sherwin said. "So I guess I should tell you that I really don't belong in Group C. I'm better than that."

"So you think you can beat me?"

"I've timed myself with puzzles. I'm fast."

"I'm sure you are."

A volunteer set the first puzzle—freshly printed on fine cotton paper—facedown on the table in front of Sherwin.

"So what happens now?" Sherwin asked.

"When they say *go*, you turn over the paper and do your puzzle. When you're finished, raise your hand, and somebody will mark your time, and then they'll collect your puzzle and check it for accuracy. And they'll measure your score against all the other C Group puzzlers."

"The woman said they'd move me up to B if I did well enough."

"Why don't you just do the first puzzle and see what happens? What's your name anyway?"

"Sherwin."

"I'm Mai. What do you do when you aren't solving puzzles?"

"I'm a writer."

"Oh. Have you written anything I might have heard of?"

"Doubtful. I wrote poems and short stories. I never sold much. And never won any awards. I wrote a couple of movies, too. But they never got made."

"What are you working on now?"

"Oh, I don't write anymore."

"Why not?"

"My talent dried up and blew away in the wind," Sherwin said. "I am the Dust Bowl."

"I'm sorry to hear that."

"I'm sorry to say it."

Sherwin had never before confessed aloud his fears that his talent was gone forever. And now that he had, he realized that he would never write again. Not like he had. Was that so bad? He'd written two decent books and two bad ones. How many people in the world had written and published anything? Because he'd stopped writing, Sherwin had been thinking of himself as a failure. But perhaps that wasn't it. Perhaps he had only been destined to be a writer for that brief period of time. After all, there must be at least one person in the world who had loved his books—who still loved his work—so perhaps that made it all worthwhile. Wasn't everything temporary anyway?

"Okay, wait, Sherwin, enough of the biography," the Korean woman said. "Here we go."

"Puzzlers," the emcee said, "start your puzzles."

Sherwin and the Korean woman, and a few hundred other puzzlers, flipped over their papers and started working. Sherwin quickly filled three Across answers and one Down, but then stalled. He read through the clues and found that he didn't know any of them offhand. He was stuck already. Thirty seconds into his first puzzle and he was frozen. Words were failing him. Again and again, they failed him. He stared blankly at his mostly empty grid for one minute and three seconds and was shocked when the Korean woman raised her hand.

"You're done?" he asked.

"You're not supposed to talk," she said.

"But you're really done that fast?"

"Yes, but that bitch up there beat me again."

Sherwin checked out of the hotel, caught a taxi to the airport, and the flight to Chicago that would connect him to the flight back home to San Francisco.

On the second leg, somewhere over Wyoming, Sherwin pulled out the *New York Times* and found the crossword. It was Saturday, so this puzzle would probably be difficult to solve. Sherwin vowed to solve it, quickly and accurately. He wanted redemption. Here, in the airplane, he was able to fill in a few boxes, but not many. The puzzle remained mostly unsolved.

He was ready to crumple the paper into a ball and stuff it into the seat pocket in front of him when he became aware that he was being watched. One row behind him, to the left and across the aisle, a man was simultaneously working the airline magazine crossword puzzle and watching Sherwin work his *New York Times* puzzle. The airline magazine puzzles were embarrassingly easy. But the man was obviously struggling and was embarrassed by his struggles.

"I'll figure this out," he said to Sherwin, "but you, man, you're working the *Times* puzzle. You must be a genius."

"Maybe," Sherwin said.

Wanting to confirm the man's opinion, Sherwin again studied the puzzle. He tentatively filled in one answer. It was wrong, surely it was wrong; ALPINE could not be the right answer. It made no sense. But it fit the squares. It put ink on the page. Sherwin felt good about that, so he filled in another answer with the wrong word. And then he filled in another. In a minute, he finished the puzzle. He'd filled nearly all the boxes with incorrect and random words like *music* and *screenwriter* and *fear* but the man behind him could not tell that Sherwin was faking it. He could only see Sherwin finishing the difficult puzzle in record time. Wow, the man thought, he's barely even reading the clues. He's a crossword machine. He's a crossword cyborg. He's a crossword killer. He's a crossword Terminator.

When Sherwin filled in the last blank, he sighed with satisfaction, folded the paper in half, and slid it into the seat pocket in front of him. Then he looked back at the man behind him and smiled. The man gave him a thumbs-up. It was such an eager and innocent gesture that Sherwin felt guilty for his deception. But then he laughed at himself, at his gift for lying.

I am a lying genius, Sherwin thought. And what is lying but a form of storytelling? Sherwin realized that he'd told a story, the first story he'd told in public for any kind of audience since he left Hollywood. But wait, did this really count as story-telling? Well, he'd entertained one man, right? And then Sherwin realized what he'd truly just done. And he roared with laughter and startled a few of his fellow passengers with the volume of his joy.

Sherwin realized that, for years, he'd been running away from a wildfire, an all-consuming inferno that had turned his words into cinder and ash, but he'd just now set an escape fire; he'd told a lie, a story, that convinced him he might be capable of putting a story on the page. Or was this all delusion? Sherwin knew there was a pen in his left inside coat pocket. He could feel it there. And there was paper everywhere on this airplane. He had ink; he could get paper. Oh, he wondered, oh, do I have the strength to begin again? Do I have the courage to step into a dark theater, hold hands with a beautiful woman, and fall back in love with my innocence?

ODE TO MIX TAPES

These days, it's too easy to make mix tapes.
    CD burners, iPods, and iTunes
        Have taken the place
    Of vinyl and cassette. And, soon
Enough, clever introverts will create
Quicker point-and-click ways to declare
    One's love, lust, friendship, and favor.
        But I miss the labor
Of making old-school mix tapes—the midair

Acrobatics of recording one song
    At a time. It sometimes took days
        To play, choose, pause,
    Ponder, record, replay, erase,
And replace. But there was no magic wand.
It was blue-collar work. A great mix tape
    Was sculpture designed to seduce
        And let the hounds loose.
A great mix tape was a three-chord parade

Led by the first song, something bold and brave,
  A heat-seeker like Prince with "Cream,"
  Or "Let's Get It On," by Marvin Gaye.
The next song was always Patsy Cline's "Sweet Dreams,"
or something by Hank. But O, the last track
  Was the vessel that contained
  The most devotion and pain
And made promises that you couldn't take back.

Roman Catholic Haiku

Humans

In 1985, while attending Gonzaga University—a Jesuit institution—students shared the dining hall with fifty or sixty nuns who lived in a dormitory-turned-convent. We students didn't think positively or negatively about this situation. We barely had any interaction with the holy women, though a few of us took to shouting, "Get thee to a nunnery!" at one another—but never at the nuns—after we took a Shakespeare class. I'm sure the nuns must have heard us shouting Hamlet's curse at one another, but being a rather scholarly bunch, they were probably more amused than insulted.

Nature

The brown recluse spider is not an aggressive spider and attacks only when hurt or threatened. Its bite, however, contains a very aggressive poison that can form a necrotizing ulcer that destroys soft tissue and sometimes bone. So this six-eyed spider is passive and dangerous. And it's strangely beautiful. It often has markings on its stomach and back that resemble violins. Yes, this spider could be thought of as a tattooed musician.

COLLISION

While waiting in the lunch line behind a nun, I noticed a brown recluse spider perched on her shoulder. I reflexively slapped the arachnid to the floor. The nun must have thought I'd slapped her in jest or cruelty because she turned and glared at me. But then I pointed at the brown recluse spider scuttling across the floor away from us. At first, the nun stepped back, but then she took two huge steps forward and crushed the spider underfoot. The nun gasped; I gasped. Mortified, she looked at me and said, "I'm sorry." And then she looked down at the mutilated spider and said, "You, too."

LOOKING GLASS

On October 5, 1877, in Idaho's Bear Paw Mountains, the starved and exhausted Nez Perce ended their two-thousand-mile flight and surrendered to General Oliver Howard and his Ninth Cavalry. When the legendary Nez Perce leader, Chief Joseph, stood and said, "My heart is sick

And
Sad.
From
Where
The
Sun
Now
Stands,

I
Will
Fight
No
More
Forever"

he thought they were his final words. He had no idea that he would live for another twenty-seven years. First, he watched hundreds of his people die of exile in Oklahoma. Then Joseph and his fellow survivors were allowed to move back to the Pacific Northwest but were forced to live on the Colville Indian Reservation, hundreds of miles away from their tribe's ancestral home in Oregon's Wallowa Valley. Exiled twice, Joseph still led his tribe into the twentieth century, though he eventually died of depression. But my grandmother, who was born on the Colville Indian Reservation, always said she remembered Joseph as a kind and peaceful man. She always said that Chief Joseph was her favorite babysitter.

Yes,
He
Would
Sit
In
His
Rocking
Chair

And
Braid
My
Grandmother's
Epic
Hair.

SALT

I wrote the obituary for the obituaries editor. Her name was Lois Andrews. Breast cancer. She was only forty-five. One in eight women get breast cancer, an epidemic. Lois's parents had died years earlier. Dad's cigarettes kept their promises. Mom's Parkinson's shook her into the ground. Lois had no siblings and had never been married. No kids. No significant other at present. No significant others in recent memory. Nobody remembered meeting one of her others. Some wondered if there had been any others. Perhaps Lois had been that rarest of holy people, the secular and chaste nun. So, yes, her sexuality was a mystery often discussed but never solved. She had many friends. All of them worked at the paper.

I wasn't her friend, not really. I was only eighteen, a summer intern at the newspaper, moving from department to department as need and boredom required, and had only spent a few days working with Lois. But she'd left a note, a handwritten will and testament, with the editor in chief, and she'd named me as the person she wanted to write her obituary.

"Why me?" I asked the chief. He was a bucket of pizza and beer tied to a broomstick.

"I don't know," he said. "It's what she wanted."

"I didn't even know her."

"She was a strange duck," he said.

I wanted to ask him how to tell the difference between strange and typical ducks. But he was a humorless white man with power, and I was a reservation Indian boy intern. I was to be admired for my ethnic tenacity but barely tolerated because of my callow youth.

"I've never written an obituary by myself," I said. During my hours at her desk, Lois had carefully supervised my work.

"It may seem bureaucratic and formal," she'd said. "But we have to be perfect. This is a sacred thing. We have to do this perfectly."

"Come on," the chief said. "What did you do when you were working with her? She taught you how to write one, didn't she?"

"Well, yeah, but—"

"Just do your best," he said and handed me her note. It was short, rather brutal, and witty. She didn't want any ceremony. She didn't want a moment of silence. Or a moment of indistinct noise, either. And she didn't want anybody to gather at a local bar and tell drunken stories about her because those stories would inevitably be romantic and false. And she'd rather be forgotten than inaccurately remembered. And she wanted me to write the obituary.

It was an honor, I guess. It would have been difficult, maybe impossible, to write a good obituary about a woman I didn't know. But she made it easy. She insisted in her letter that I use the standard fill-in-the-blanks form.

"If it was good enough for others," she'd written, "it is good enough for me."

A pragmatic and lonely woman, sure. And serious about her work. But, trust me, she was able to tell jokes without insulting the dead. At least, not directly.

That June, a few days before she went on the medical leave that she'd never return from, Lois had typed *surveyed* instead of *survived* in the obituary for a locally famous banker. That error made it past the copy editors and was printed: *Mr. X is surveyed by his family and friends.*

Mr. X's widow called Lois to ask about the odd word choice.

"I'm sorry," Lois said. She was mortified. It was the only serious typo of her career. "It was my error. It's entirely my fault. I apologize. I will correct it for tomorrow's issue."

"Oh, no, please don't," the widow said. "My husband would have loved it. He was a poet. Never published or anything like that. But he loved poems. And that word, *survey*—well, it might be accidental, but it's poetry, I think. I mean, my husband would have been delighted to know that his family and friends were surveying him at the funeral."

And so a surprised and delighted Lois spent the rest of the day thinking of verbs that more accurately reflected our interactions with the dead.

Mr. X is assailed by his family and friends.
Mr. X is superseded by his family and friends.
Mr. X is superimposed by his family and friends.
Mr. X is sensationalized by his family and friends.
Mr. X is shadowboxed by his family and friends.

Lois laughed as she composed her imaginary obituaries. I'd never seen her laugh that much, and I suspected that very few people had seen her react that strongly to anything. She wasn't remote or strained, she was just private. And so her laughter—her public joy—was frankly erotic. Though I'd always thought of her as a sexy librarian—with her wire-rimmed glasses and curly brown hair and serious panty hose and suits—I'd never really thought of going to bed with her. Not to any serious degree. I was eighteen, so I fantasized about having sex with nearly every woman I saw, but I hadn't obsessed about Lois. Not really. I'd certainly noticed that her calves were a miracle of muscle—her best feature—but I'd only occasionally thought of kissing my way up and down her legs. But at that moment, as she laughed about death, I had to shift my legs to hide my erection.

"Hey, kid," she said, "when you die, how do you want your friends and family to remember you?"

"Jeez," I said. "I don't want to think about that stuff. I'm eighteen."

"Oh, so young," she said. "So young and handsome. You're going to be very popular with the college girls."

I almost whimpered. But I froze, knowing that the slightest movement, the softest brush of my pants against my skin, would cause me to orgasm.

Forgive me, I was only a kid.

"Ah, look at you," Lois said. "You're blushing."

And so I grabbed a random file off her desk and ran. I made my escape. But, oh, I was in love with the obituaries editor. And she—well, she taught me how to write an obituary.

And so this is how I wrote hers:

Lois Andrews, age 45, of Spokane, died Friday,
August 24, 1985, at Sacred Heart Hospital.

There will be no funeral service. She donated her
body to Washington State University. An only child,
Lois Anne Andrews was born January 16, 1940, at
Sacred Heart Hospital, to Martin and Betsy
(Harrison) Andrews. She never married. She was the
obituaries editor at the *Spokesman-Review* for twenty-
two years. She is survived by her friends and col-
leagues at the newspaper.

Yes, that was the story of her death. It was not enough. I felt
morally compelled to write a few more sentences, as if those
extra words would somehow compensate for what had been a
brief and solitary life.

I was also bothered that Lois had donated her body to
science. Of course, her skin and organs would become train-
ing tools for doctors and scientists, and that was absolutely
vital, but the whole process still felt disrespectful to me. I
thought of her, dead and naked, lying on a gurney while dozens of students stuck their hands inside of her. It seemed—
well, pornographic. But I also knew that my distaste was
cultural.

Indians respect dead bodies even more than the live ones.

Of course, I never said anything. I was young and frightened and craved respect and its ugly cousin, approval, so I did
as I was told. And that's why, five days after Lois's death and
a few minutes after the editor in chief had told me I would be

writing the obituaries until they found "somebody official," I found myself sitting at her desk.

"What am I supposed to do first?" I asked the chief.

"Well, she must have unfiled files and unwritten obits and unmailed letters."

"Okay, but where?"

"I don't know. It was *her* desk."

This was in the paper days, and Lois kept five tall filing cabinets stuffed with her job.

"I don't know what to do," I said, panicked.

"Jesus, boy," the editor in chief said. "If you want to be a journalist, you'll have to work under pressure. Jesus. And this is hardly any pressure at all. All these people are dead. The dead will not pressure you."

I stared at him. I couldn't believe what he was saying. He seemed so cruel. He was a cruel duck, that's what he was.

"Jesus," he said yet again, and grabbed a folder off the top of the pile. "Start with this one."

He handed me the file and walked away. I wanted to shout at him that he'd said Jesus three times in less than fifteen seconds. I wasn't a Christian and didn't know much about the definition of blasphemy, but it seemed like he'd committed some kind of sin.

But I kept my peace, opened the file, and read the handwritten letter inside. A woman had lost her husband. Heart attack. And she wanted to write the obituary and run his picture. She included her phone number. I figured it was okay to call her. So I did.

"Hello?" she said. Her name was Mona.

"Oh, hi," I said. "I'm calling from the *Spokesman-Review*. About your—uh, late husband?"

"Oh. Oh, did you get my letter? I'm so happy you called. I wasn't sure if anybody down there would pay attention to me."

"This is sacred," I said, remembering Lois's lessons. "We take this very seriously."

"Oh, well, that's good—that's great—and, well, do you think it will be okay for me to write the obituary? I'm a good writer. And I'd love to run my husband's photo—his name was Dean—I'd love to run his photo with the—with his—with my remembrance of him."

I had no idea if it was okay for her to write the obituary. And I believed that the newspaper generally ran only the photographs of famous dead people. But then I looked at the desktop and noticed Lois's neatly written notes trapped beneath the glass. I gave praise for her organizational skills.

"Okay, okay," I said, scanning the notes. "Yes. Yes, it's okay if you want to write the obituary yourself."

I paused and then read aloud the official response to such a request.

"Because we understand, in your time of grieving, that you want your loved one to be honored with the perfect words—"

"Oh, that's lovely."

"—but, and we're truly sorry about this, it will cost you extra," I said.

"Oh," she said. "Oh, I didn't know that. How much extra?"

"Fifty dollars."

"Wow, that's a lot of money."

"Yes," I said. It was one-fifth of my monthly rent.

"And how about running the photograph?" Mona asked. "How much extra does that cost?"

"It depends on the size of the photo."

"How much is the smallest size?"

"Fifty dollars, as well."

"So it will be one hundred dollars to do this for my husband?"

"Yes."

"I don't know if I can afford it. I'm a retired schoolteacher on a fixed income."

"What did you teach?" I asked.

"I taught elementary school—mostly second grade—at Meadow Hills for forty-five years. I taught three generations." She was proud, even boastful. "I'll have you know that I taught the grandchildren of three of my original students."

"Well, listen," I said, making an immediate and inappropriate decision to fuck the duck in chief. "We have a special rate for—uh, retired public employees. So the rate for your own obituary and your husband's photograph is—uh, let's say twenty dollars. Does that sound okay?"

"Twenty dollars? Twenty dollars? I can do twenty dollars. Yes, that's lovely. Oh, thank you, thank you."

"You're welcome, ma'am. So—uh, tell me, when do you want this to run?"

"Well, I told my daughters and sons that it would run tomorrow."

"Tomorrow?"

"Yes, the funeral is tomorrow. I really want this to run on the same day. Is that okay? Will that be possible?"

I had no idea if it was possible. "Let me talk to the boys down in the print room," I said, as if I knew them. "And I'll call you back in a few minutes, okay?"

"Oh, yes, yes, I'll be waiting by the phone."

We said our good-byes and I slumped in my chair. In Lois's chair. What had I done? I'd made a promise I could not keep. I counted to one hundred, trying to find a cool center, and walked over to the chief's office.

"What do you want?" he asked.

"I think I screwed up."

"Well, isn't that a surprise," he said. I wanted to punch the sarcasm out of his throat.

"This woman—her husband died," I said. "And she wanted to write the obituary and run his photo—"

"That costs extra."

"I know. I read that on Lois's desk. But I read incorrectly, I think."

"How incorrectly?"

"Well, I think it's supposed to cost, like, one hundred dollars to run the obit and the size photo she wants—"

"How much did you tell her it would cost?"

"Twenty."

"So you gave her an eighty-percent discount?"

"I guess."

He stared at me. Judged me. He'd once been a Pulitzer finalist for a story about a rural drug syndicate.

"And there's more," I said.

"Yes?" His anger was shrinking his vocabulary.

"I told her we'd run it tomorrow."

"Jesus," he said. "Damn it, kid."

I think he wanted to fire me, to throw me out of his office, out of his building, out of his city and country. I suddenly realized that he was grieving for Lois, that he was angry about her death. Of course he was. They had worked together for two decades. They were friends. So I tried to forgive him for his short temper. And I did forgive him, a little.

"I'm sorry," I said.

"Well, shit on a rooster," he said, and leaned back in his chair. "Listen. I know this is a tough gig here. This is not your job. I know that. But this is a newspaper and we measure the world by column inches, okay? We have to make tough decisions about what can fit and what cannot fit. And by telling this woman—this poor woman—that she could have this space tomorrow, you have fucked with the shape of my world, okay?"

"Yes, sir," I said.

He ran his fingers through his hair (my father did the same thing when he was pissed), made a quick decision, picked up his phone, and made the call.

"Hey, Charlie, it's me," he said. "Do we have any room for another obituary? With a photo?"

I could hear the man screaming on the other end.

"I know, I know," the chief said. "But this is an important one. It's a family thing."

The chief listened to more screaming, then hung up on the other guy.

"All right," he said. "The woman gets one column inch for the obit."

"That's not much," I said.

"She's going to have to write a haiku, isn't she?"

I wanted to tell him that haikus were not supposed to be elegies, but then I realized that I wasn't too sure about that literary hypothesis.

"What do I do now?" I asked.

"We need the obit and the photo by three o'clock."

It was almost one.

"How do I get them?" I asked.

"Well, you could do something crazy like get in a car, drive to this woman's house, pick up the obit and the photo, and bring them back here."

"I don't have a car," I said.

"Do you have a driver's license?"

"Yes."

"Well, then, why don't you go sign a vehicle out of the car pool and do your fucking job?"

I fled. Obtained the car. And while cursing Lois and her early death, and then apologizing to Lois for cursing her, I drove up Maple to the widow's small house on Francis. A green house with a white fence that was maybe one foot tall. A useless fence. It couldn't keep out anything.

I rang the doorbell and waited a long time for the woman—Mona, her name was Mona—to answer. She was scrawny, thin-haired, dark for a white woman. At least eighty years old. Maybe ninety. Maybe older than that. I did the math. Geronimo was still alive when this woman was born. An old raven, I thought. No, too small to be a raven. She was a starling.

"Hello," she said.

"Hi, Mona," I said. "I'm from the *Spokesman;* we talked on the phone."

"Oh, yes, oh, yes, please come in."

I followed her inside into the living room. She slowly, painfully, sat on a wooden chair. She was too weak and frail to lower herself into a soft chair, I guess. I sat on her couch. I looked around the room and realized that every piece of furniture, every painting, every knickknack and candlestick, was older than me. Most of the stuff was probably older than my parents. I saw photographs of Mona, a man I assumed was her husband, and five or six children, and a few dozen grandchildren. Her children and grandchildren, I guess. Damn, her children were older than my parents. Her grandchildren were older than me.

"You have a nice house," I said.

"My husband and I lived here for sixty years. We raised five children here."

"Where are your children now?"

"Oh, they live all over the country. But they're all flying in tonight and tomorrow for the funeral. They loved their father. Do you love your father?"

My father was a drunken liar.

"Yes," I said. "I love him very much."

"That's good, you're a good son. A very good son."

She smiled at me. I realized she'd forgotten why I was there.

"Ma'am, about the obituary and the photograph?"

"Yes?" she said, still confused.

"We need them, the obituary you wrote for your husband, and his photograph?"

And then she remembered.

"Oh, yes, oh, yes, I have them right here in my pocket."

She handed me the photograph and the obit. And yes, it was clumsily written and mercifully short. The man in the photograph was quite handsome. A soldier in uniform. Black hair, blue eyes. I wondered if his portrait had been taken before or after he'd killed somebody.

"My husband was a looker, wasn't he?" she asked.

"Yes, very much so."

"I couldn't decide which photograph to give you. I mean, I thought I might give you a more recent one. To show you what he looks like now. He's still very handsome. But then I thought, No, let's find the most beautiful picture of them all. Let the world see my husband at his best. Don't you think that's romantic?"

"Yes, you must have loved him very much," I said.

"Oh, yes, he was ninety percent perfect. Nobody's all perfect, of course. But he was close, he was very close."

Her sentiment was brutal.

"Listen, ma'am," I said. "I'm sorry, but I have to get these photographs back to the newspaper if they're going to run on time."

"Oh, don't worry, young man, there's no rush."

Now I was confused. "But I thought the funeral was tomorrow?" I asked.

"Oh, no, silly, I buried my husband six months ago. In Veterans' Cemetery. He was at D-Day."

"And your children?"

"Oh, they were here for the funeral, but they went away."

But she looked around the room as if she could still see her kids. Or maybe she was remembering them as they had been, the children who'd indiscriminately filled the house and then, just as indiscriminately, had moved away and into their own houses. Or maybe everything was ghosts, ghosts, ghosts. She scared me. Maybe this house was lousy with ghosts. I was afraid that Lois's ghost was going to touch me on the shoulder and gently correct my errors.

"Mona, are you alone here?" I asked. I didn't want to know the answer.

"No, no—well, yes, I suppose. But my Henry, he's buried in the backyard."

"Henry?"

"My cat. Oh, my beloved cat."

And then she told me about Henry and his death. The poor cat, just as widowed as Mona, had fallen into a depression after her husband's death. Cat and wife mourned together.

"You know," she said. "I read once that grief can cause cancer. I think it's true. At least, it's true for cats. Because that's what my Henry had, cancer of the blood. Cats get it all the time. They see a lot of death, they do."

And so she, dependent on the veterinarian's kindness and charity, had arranged for her Henry to be put down.

"What's that big word for killing cats?" she asked me.

"Euthanasia," I said.

"Yes, that's it. That's the word. It's kind of a pretty word, isn't it? It sounds pretty, don't you think?"

"Yes."

"Such a pretty word for such a sad and lonely thing," she said.

"Yes, it is," I said.

"You can name your daughter Euthanasia and nobody would even notice if they didn't know what the word meant."

"I suppose," I said.

"Euthanasia," she said. "It would be a beautiful name for a beautiful girl."

Shit, I imagined Princess Euthanasia, daughter of Tsar Nicolas, riding her pony over the snowy Siberian plains.

"My cat was too sick to live," Mona said.

And then she told me how she'd held Henry as the vet injected him with the death shot. And, oh, how she cried when Henry's heart and breath slowed and stopped. He was gone, gone, gone. And so she brought him home, carried him into the backyard, and laid him beside the hole she'd paid a neighbor boy to dig. That neighbor boy was probably fifty years old.

"I prayed for a long time," she said. "I wanted God to know that my cat deserved to be in Heaven. And I didn't want Henry to be in cat heaven. Not at all. I wanted Henry to go find my husband. I want them both to be waiting for me."

And so she prayed for hours. Who can tell the exact time at such moments? And then she kneeled beside her cat. And that was painful because her knees were so old, so used—like the ancient sedan in the garage—and she pushed her Henry into the grave and poured salt over him.

"I read once," she said, "that the Egyptians used to cover dead bodies with salt. It helps people get to Heaven quicker. That's what I read."

When she poured the salt on her cat, a few grains dropped and burned in his eyes.

"And let me tell you," she said. "I almost fell in that grave when my Henry meowed. Just a little one. I barely heard it. But it was there. I put my hand on his chest and his little heart was beating. Just barely. But it was beating. I couldn't believe it. The salt brought him back to life."

Shit, I thought, the damn vet hadn't injected enough death juice into the cat. Shit, shit, shit.

"Oh, that's awful," I said.

"No, I was happy. My cat was alive. Because of the salt. So I called my doctor—"

"You mean you called the vet?"

"No, I called my doctor, Ed Marashi, and I told him that it was a miracle, that the salt brought Henry back to life."

I wanted to scream at her senile hope. I wanted to run to Lois's grave and cover her with salt so she'd rise, replace me, and be forced to hear this story. This was her job; this was her responsibility.

"And let me tell you," the old woman said. "My doctor was amazed, too, so he said he'd call the vet and they'd both be over, and it wasn't too long before they were both in my home. Imagine! Two doctors on a house call. That doesn't happen anymore, does it?"

It happens when two graceful men want to help a fragile and finite woman.

And so she told me that the doctors went to work on the cat. And, oh, how they tried to bring him back all the way, but there just wasn't enough salt in the world to make it happen. So the doctors helped her sing and pray and bury her Henry. And, oh, yes—Dr. Marashi had sworn to her that he'd tried to help her husband with salt.

"Dr. Marashi said he poured salt on my husband," she said. "But it didn't work. There are some people too sick to be salted."

She looked around the room as if she expected her husband and cat to materialize. How well can you mourn if you continually forget that the dead are dead?

I needed to escape.

"I'm really sorry, ma'am," I said. "I really am. But I have to get back to the newspaper with these."

"Is that my husband's photograph?" she asked.

"Yes."

"And is that his obituary?"

"Yes," I said. "It's the one you wrote."

"I remember, I remember."

She studied the artifacts in my hands.

"Can I have them back?" she asked.

"Excuse me?"

"The photo, and my letter, that's all I have to remember my husband. He died, you know?"

"Yes, I know," I said.

"He was at D-Day."

"If I give you these back," I said. "I won't be able to run them in the newspaper."

"Oh, I don't want them in the newspaper," she said. "My husband was a very private man."

Ah, Lois, I thought, you never told me about this kind of death.

"I have to go now," I said. I wanted to crash through the door and run away from this house fire.

"Okay, okay. Thank you for visiting," she said. "Will you come back? I love visitors."

"Yes," I said. I lied. I knew I should call somebody about her dementia. She surely couldn't take care of herself anymore. I knew I should call the police or her doctor or find her children and tell them. I knew I had responsibilities to her—to this grieving and confused stranger—but I was young and terrified.

So I left her on her porch. She was still waving when I turned the corner. Ah, Lois, I thought, are you with me, are you with me? I drove the newspaper's car out of the city and onto the freeway. I drove for three hours to the shore of Soap Lake, an inland sea heavy with iron, calcium, and salt. For thousands of years, my indigenous ancestors had traveled here to be healed. They're all gone now, dead by disease and self-destruction. Why had they believed so strongly in this magic water when it never protected them for long? When it might not have protected them at all? But you, Lois, you were never afraid of death, were you? You laughed and played. And you honored the dead with your brief and serious prayers.

Standing on the shore, I prayed for my dead. I praised them. I stupidly hoped the lake would heal my small wounds. Then I stripped off my clothes and waded naked into the water.

Jesus, I don't want to die today or tomorrow, but I don't want to live forever.

Food Chain

This is my will:

Bury me
In an anthill.

After one week
Of this feast,

Set the ants on fire.
Make me a funeral pyre.

Let my smoke rise
Into the eyes

Of those crows
On the telephone wire.

Startle those birds
Into flight

With my last words:
I loved my life.

11-09

F   Alexie, Sherman
         War dances.